THE RED HOODIE

AN AMBER MCNEIL MYSTERY

SANDRA NIKOLAI

"All wolves are not of the same sort."
Charles Perrault, author (1628–1703)

1

The scent of polished wood floors and freshly painted walls couldn't offset the musty smell of eight hundred cold cases waiting for justice. As I ran my hand along the rows of competing bankers boxes at the Montreal Police Service headquarters, it was hard to focus.

The image of a little girl's hand popped into my mind. It vanished in the next instant. An uneasy and eerie feeling settled in the pit of my stomach, like it did whenever I lingered in the storage room.

My mind raced, overwhelmed with frantic screams and disturbing images as my fingers flitted across more boxes. Were the victims' cries for help all in my head?

Not at all.

I come from a line of empaths, so these perceptions were real to me. My psychic ability to get an impression when touching an object was an advantage in my job as consultant to police investigators. My sensory talents had been a curse for twenty-five years, but now I could finally harness them for good.

There was one problem, though. It was hard to remain

objective and not panic when I examined case evidence, like shocking crime scene photos and personal articles that had belonged to the victim. It wasn't only about the physical evidence. My perceptions, mental images or feelings that I experienced without warning, often left me gasping for air. Learning how to control my emotions was an ongoing struggle, but I was determined to win. Why? Because I truly believed it was my duty to help these victims.

I paused at a box marked *Marie Troy, 1968* on the bottom shelf. I knelt down, balancing on my two-inch heels to get a closer look. As I ran my fingers across the letters, a bright red flash clouded my vision. Whenever I experienced one of these strange visual disturbances, it signaled to me that I'd found the case I needed to work on. I pulled the box from the shelf and carried it out of the storage room.

My heels clicked as I walked down the hallway to the department's renovated office. The top brass had recognized our recent investigative success and rewarded us by converting our former makeshift office into a suitable workplace. It now held a conference room, a small kitchen, and desks for each member of our newly formed cold case unit.

Corey Reed and Nadia Paquin, recent university graduates, were information officers who gathered, validated, and trans-mitted data regarding criminal cases. One of their tasks was to transfer the information stored in boxed cold case files to the police computer database. Seated at a desk facing Nadia, the gangly man was in a heated discussion with her about some-thing technical. Her wavy brown hair, a couple of shades lighter than my dark brunette, softened her usual deadpan expression as she stared at him. Both ignored me as I went by.

I strode by Lieutenant Albert Payton's glass-walled office. He nodded at me before continuing his conversation on the phone. The lieutenant reminded us daily that the pressure was on. The department constantly faced the threat of drastic budget cuts. We had to solve a quota of cases to maintain operations, or else our unit would be eliminated. Of course, the regular members of the force, like Corey and Nadia, would simply get reassigned. As a civilian, there were no other roles for me.

Detective Sergeant Ryan Baxter, the handsome thirtysomething lead investigator and criminal profiler, sat facing me. Our computers separated us and allowed for some privacy, though the top of his thick brown hair alerted me whenever he was at his desk.

Detective Sergeant Matt Gallo sat to the left of us. In his mid-forties and recently divorced, he was an experienced investigator Ryan had recruited from homicide a week ago. While Matt spoke on the phone in a hushed tone, he flipped through reports in another cold case file. Across from him was an empty desk, which the lieutenant would fill with another investigator if we succeeded in solving more cases. *If* was a cautionary word in our unit.

Aside from Ryan and the lieutenant, no one else in the unit knew about my psychic gift. To protect me from curious minds, as well as devious ones, the lieutenant had suggested from the start that we keep it a secret among us. I preferred it that way. To the rest of the team, I was introduced as a consultant "with unique observation skills."

I was thankful that our unit was separated from homicide and other police departments in the building. It limited my exposure to the negative emotions and energy triggered by other detectives working grisly murder cases, interviewing traumatized witnesses, and grilling suspected perpetrators.

Ryan craned his neck around the computer monitor. "Good morning, Amber." He smiled and winked at me as I set the bankers box down on my desk.

I felt a gush of warmth inside and returned a brief smile, then hastily sat down. A nervous glance around confirmed that no one else had noticed his wink or the signs of attraction between us.

Our relationship had developed into a romantic one after

we'd worked on our first cold case together. I was thrilled about it, but was he *the one*? I didn't know. In any case, we'd agreed to take it slowly.

There was one clear obstacle to our relationship, though. An intimate rapport between staff within the same police unit was prohibited. If it were discovered, I would be easy to terminate, but Ryan had more than a decade of experience as a police officer. I didn't want to be responsible for his reassignment to another unit or worse: the loss of his job. Neither of us wanted that, so we agreed to hide our relationship from colleagues, which made it more exciting in a way.

We had another reason for keeping our relationship a secret: We'd put a lot of effort into helping the lieutenant set up the new unit. It was our baby, so to speak, and we were totally devoted to furthering its success. We'd hate to give it all up, especially when the unit was in its infancy and the future was so promising.

Working on criminal cases at police headquarters was serious business. *Deadly* serious business. My personal relationship with Ryan didn't figure into the equation. I had to give the job my entire focus if I wanted to keep it. Period.

If there was one person I especially didn't want to disappoint, it was Chief Inspector Ted Tremblay, who happened to be my uncle. He believed that my special abilities would be a game changer, that my insights would help to solve cold cases and keep the unit running. That he'd recommended me for the consultant job was another well-kept secret known only to Ryan, the lieutenant, and me. I couldn't imagine what would happen if anyone else found out!

Matt stood up and approached me, the scent of his spicy aftershave invading my nostrils. "Can I get anyone a hot coffee on this cool October morning?" He eyed me in particular.

I didn't have to be psychic to see he was trying hard to please me. We'd spoken briefly since he joined the unit, but it was obvious he wanted to get to know me on a more personal level. That would never happen.

"No, thanks, Matt," I said. Even as I looked away, I felt his eyes roaming over my body.

When Ryan also declined his offer too, Matt sauntered off toward the kitchen.

My confidence had soared the other day when Ryan suggested that I pick the next cold case we'd work on. He trusted my insights. But although I was eager to review the files with him, insecurities crept in once in a while. Would he accept my choice?

"Which case called out to you this time, Amber?" Ryan rounded the corner of my desk, his tall muscular form one of the reasons I was so drawn to him.

"Marie Troy, 1968."

He stood closer to me and gently squeezed my hand.

I pulled my hand away and flipped my hair over my shoulder, annoyed that he'd risk such an affectionate gesture. What if another coworker had noticed?

"Uh...sorry," he whispered. "Sometimes I can't help myself." He pulled up a chair beside me, his demeanor now all businesslike. "Let's see what we have here."

I removed the lid from Marie Troy's bankers box and dug out the investigative file. Inside was a faded Polaroid photo of an eight-year-old girl with blonde hair and blue eyes. She wore a red hoodie over a school uniform and held a plaid schoolbag. As I held the photo, a stream of images sped through my mind: a man's hand...a narrow road...a stifling, enclosed space. My breath caught in my throat.

Ryan had witnessed my sensitive reactions to case evidence before. "Are you okay, Amber?" he asked in a quiet voice.

I told him about my perceptions. "I think I'm sensing all of this through Marie."

"Those images could be clues." He picked up a witness report from the file and read it. "Marie's mother states she believed her daughter went missing on her way to school that morning." He reached for other reports and scanned them. "Oh, hell!"

"What's wrong?"

"There's no follow-up on any of the witness statements. Fingerprints were lifted but not verified. I'd hate to think that past investigators did sloppy work. Maybe budget cuts stopped them in their tracks. Damn!" He tossed the reports on the desk.

I'd rarely seen him get this angry. Exasperation sparked from him like a crackling fire. I shuddered.

"Sorry, I didn't mean to dump my frustrations on you," he said in a soft voice.

"This isn't like you, Ryan. What's the matter?"

"It's this case." He retrieved the pile of reports. "Here we have reports about a little girl who disappeared in broad daylight. From what I've read so far, we have no leads. Somebody must have seen something."

I peered closer at the photo of Marie. A tiny round object hung from a gold chain around her neck.

All of a sudden, pain gripped me, and a pang shot through my chest. "No!" I dropped the photo and leaned over.

Ryan put his hands on my shoulders to steady me. "Just breathe."

I drew in a lungful and hastily clasped the amethyst cluster in my pocket to calm my nerves. It was a gift from my Aunt Elaine, Uncle Ted's wife. She shared the same psychic lineage as me. The crystal was her way of protecting me from a job she considered too severe for the sensitivities of empaths like us. I clutched it, sensing tranquility flowing through me again.

Nadia ran up to me. "Are you okay, Amber?"

"Uh...yes, I'm fine." Embarrassed, I fished for an excuse. "I-I felt a bit dizzy, that's all."

"Are you sure?" Her eyes searched mine.

"Yes."

"Can I get you something? A coffee?"

I'd have grabbed any opportunity to stop her curiosity in its tracks, but I had to be truthful. "No, thanks."

"Are you really sure?" Nadia's perplexed stare lingered on me.

"We're good here," Ryan said to her.

"Okay." Nadia hesitated, then turned and walked away.

Ryan waited until she was out of earshot. "What is it, Amber? What did you see?"

"It's more about what I felt," I whispered. "Marie suffered a lot when she died."

"You actually sensed that?"

"Yes, but only a second of it."

Ryan's phone beeped. He glanced at the screen. "I have a meeting with the lieutenant. He wants an update on the status of our cases."

"Budget cuts on the agenda?"

"I hope not. I'll review Marie's file with you later. Can you prepare a summary of the investigative events and reports for me? It looks like a challenging case. Good choice." He slipped into his jacket and headed for the conference room.

Encouraged, I pressed on.

The date on the witness statements indicated it was a cool spring day when eight-year-old Marie Troy disappeared. One report stated that Bernadette Troy, her mother, had asked Marie to bring a jar of soup to her sick grandmother before going to school. As was the little girl's habit, she walked along the back alley to her grandmother's home a few doors over. In another report, her grandmother confirmed that Marie delivered the soup and then left right away. It didn't state whether she left by the back door or the front door on her way to school. The path she took might have made a difference.

Regardless, Marie never got there.

Police had interviewed Allen Corbin, Marie's stepfather. After Allen married Bernadette, they had a son named Tim but separated years later. The police database had turned up nothing criminal on Allen. He'd been away on business and returned to Montreal the day Marie went missing. Details of the man's schedule were sketchy or incomplete.

Investigators had also spoken with Gaston Belair, a neighbor who lived on the same street as the Troy family. He saw Marie leave for school as usual that morning before he drove off to work. His supervisor at Torg Construction confirmed Gaston had clocked in at noon and worked on a job most of the day. I took note of the fact his morning hours weren't accounted for.

As for other reports on file, no pertinent information was obtained from Sarina Bruno, a babysitter who lived on the next street, and Judy White, the young friend who usually accompanied Marie to and from school.

The last report was from an unnamed neighbor. He told police he'd found Marie's schoolbag and lunchbox on top of a garbage pile in the back alley that morning. From the schoolbag, he'd pulled out a notebook with a name on it but hadn't recognized it. He handed the items to the police later that afternoon when they made the rounds to interview residents. That he'd probably contaminated the evidence by handling it crossed my mind. Investigators hadn't noted his name, so there was no way to contact him. As Ryan had pointed out, fingerprints had been lifted from the evidence, but there was no follow-up.

I studied a Polaroid photo of the Troy residence. Typical of multi-family dwellings in the 1950s, a short driveway led from the alley behind the home to a single-car garage that flanked the backyard. Another photo showed a well-kept, grassy backyard and black wrought-iron railing that spiraled up to the first-, second-, and third-floor apartments of the red brick residence. A similar railing skirted the front of the building.

Also included was a hand-drawn map that showed the path Marie took from her home to the elementary school several blocks away. Investigators had drawn a line from the back door of her home and along the alley. Had police confirmed that specific path with a reliable source? It didn't matter. Ryan and I would have to interview every witness again anyway.

I reached into the bankers box for an evidence bag. It held a white hairbrush with pink roses on the handle. Strands of blonde hair clung to the bristles. As I held the bag, I captured an image of a young girl, smiling, her blonde hair tied back in a ponytail. It was Marie.

The next evidence bag I pulled out contained a metal lunchbox with Charlie Brown, Lucy, and Snoopy from the cast of Peanuts repeated on the front and back. As I held the bag, an image of three little girls in school uniforms eating and giggling around a lunch table popped into my thoughts, then vanished.

I dug into the box to retrieve the evidence bag that held Marie's schoolbag. The canvas bag had a red and black plaid pattern with a red plastic handle and two front buckles. A common design in the 1960s, it was the same as the schoolbag in her photo. A smaller evidence bag held two pencils, an eraser, a notebook, and a wood ruler. I studied the notebook. Marie's full name was neatly printed in block letters on the cover.

I was placing the schoolbag back in the bankers box when a chill ran through my body. My fingertips tingled, and pain shot through my right hand. I felt as if the schoolbag had been ripped out of my grasp. I dropped it, but not before another insight hit me: the shadowy, unshaven face of a man. The perpetrator! He was still alive!

I'd had a similar perception about another abductor when Ryan and I were investigating the Vicky Johnson cold case. Since five-year-old Vicky had lived in the same area as me twenty years ago, I'd felt a personal connection to the case. More so because I was about the same age as her when she was kidnapped. Sadly, my parents were killed by an intruder in our home months before Vicky's kidnapping. I was spared their fate, though I've carried the guilt since then.

That brutal childhood event had left me gasping in my sleep from nightmares more often than I cared to admit to my shrink or to Ryan. He'd guided me through Vicky's investigation and reassured me that the terrifying dreams would pass with time. I trusted him. After all, he had firsthand experience investigating hardcore criminals in homicide cases and had survived with his mental faculties intact. Yet the nightmares persisted.

Despite the lingering trauma, I vowed to stick with the job. All I needed to do was control my emotions so that I could remain detached when reviewing evidence or interviewing suspects. Only then could I attain a higher level of interpreting my psychic perceptions correctly.

It wasn't an easy task for an empath by any means, but the outcome was what truly mattered to me. When I initially took the job, success in solving cases was my way of thanking Uncle Ted and Aunt Elaine who'd raised me after my parents were murdered and paid for my university education. Although a Bachelor of Arts degree was nowhere on the list of requirements for the job, a quest for justice drove my motivation. I could use my psychic abilities to apprehend killers, get restitution for the unfortunate victims, and obtain closure for their long-suffering families. A winning situation.

I scanned the reports in Marie Troy's file again. No body. No crime scene. No suspects. The handful of witness statements offered no leads. Reports and informal notes were incomplete, as if the investigation had come to a sudden halt. Ryan was right. More recent crimes and limited time and resources probably meant no additional legwork had been devoted to Marie's case. Like other similar cases that occurred years ago, it had gone cold. We were starting from scratch.

The scant evidence on hand put Ryan and me on an even par. Even though we didn't always agree on how to decipher the data. Ryan, based on his profiling skills and logical analyses, and me, relying on my unpredictable psychic perceptions. We'd learned to compromise. As team players, my extrasensory skills complemented his experience in dealing with homicide cases.

What mattered to me most of all was that he recognized the value of my gift. But since we approached each case so differently, would he continue to trust my psychic insights?

The big picture offered a greater challenge. Constantly aware that our work was a race against time, would we be able to keep the unit operating?

The answer was right in front of us. If we wanted to save our jobs, we needed to bring cold cases back to life.

2

———

I was alone in the office when Ryan returned from his meeting with the lieutenant. He walked over to my desk and closed the space between us. "I have news. No anticipated budget cuts. Plus we get a dedicated dispatcher from homicide to handle incoming calls on the Info-Crime line during off-hours."

"That's a relief."

"Yeah." He smiled and edged closer. "I didn't have a chance to mention this earlier. I was glad we got together at your place last night."

"Me too." I stood, looked up into his dark eyes, and held back the urge to wrap my arms around him.

"Watching reruns of that comedy show took my mind off work. I wish I could have stayed longer." His lingering gaze told me he was hungry for more. He pulled me close.

"Be careful. Someone might walk in."

Ryan scanned the office. "The lieutenant is at another meeting. Matt is out investigating witnesses for his case. Nadia and Corey are having coffee in the kitchen. The coast is clear. We have a few seconds together."

His kiss made my heart thump faster. I kept my voice low. "Let's not risk everything, Ryan."

"Okay." He pulled away a second before Nadia stepped into the office with Corey right behind her, coffee mugs in their hands.

Oh no! Had she seen Ryan and me in an embrace?

Nadia gave us a brief smile, then set her coffee down and settled in her chair.

Was that an innocent smile or a knowing smile? I couldn't tell. Nadia's slender face had already taken on its usual blank expression as she stared at her computer screen.

My attention shifted to my work. I sat down and opened Marie Troy's file.

Following my lead, Ryan pulled up a chair next to me and slid into his business mode. He motioned to the file on my desk. "What have you got?"

As he'd requested, I recapped the events and witness statements for him. Not that there was much there. More thought-provoking were the insights I perceived from the items in Marie's bankers box. I handed him my notes describing them.

His eyes lit up and he whispered, "You got insights about a potential abductor from holding Marie's schoolbag? I'm impressed."

"He's old but alive."

"It's a start. At least we're not chasing a ghost."

"Even so, I can't help but draw similarities between Marie's case and Vicky's." I paused. "And mine."

Ryan leaned forward and said with compassion, "Amber, if this case triggers painful memories about your parents, we can work on another one."

Even though Marie's disappearance—yet another missing child case—brought back guilty feelings about my survival, I was determined to stay focused. "No. I'm not going to start feeling sorry for myself again. I need to work through this case on my own terms. I can do it. I know I can."

Ryan hesitated but then conceded. "Fair enough." He picked up the photos and hand-drawn map of Marie's path to school. "I'll put these up." He moved to the far wall and pinned them to a section of the evidence board, or crazy wall, as police investigators called it. He picked up the dry erase marker and wrote Marie Troy's name and age under her photo, then sat back down. "There's something about the statement that Marie's mother gave the police. I question the time lapse before she realized her kid was missing." He frowned.

"It was due to a domino effect of errors." I reached for the file and dug out a sheet of paper with handwriting on it. "A former investigator reported that Marie had a substitute home-room teacher that day. Unfortunately, she forgot to take atten-dance of the thirty-three pupils in the classroom."

"So Marie's absence went unnoticed. According to the school's practice, it means they didn't contact her mother to find out why Marie hadn't shown up."

"Right. When Marie didn't return home that afternoon, her mother called the school and then the police." I recalled another point. "One more incident contributed to the domino effect earlier in the day. Marie usually met a friend who accom-panied her to and from school every day. She was two years older than Marie. Sort of a big sister. When Marie didn't meet up with her that morning, her friend thought she was sick and had stayed home."

"So her friend went off to school without her." Ryan passed a hand over a clean-shaven chin. "Like I said earlier, somebody must have seen something."

"I agree. How easy would it be for a stranger to grab a little girl in an alley during the day without anyone hearing her scream for help?"

"Unless the alley wasn't where she was abducted. Or she knew her abductor." Ryan sat back in his chair. "Did you notice any other inconsistencies in the reports?"

"Yes. It's not stated whether Marie left her grandmother's by the back door or the front door after she dropped off the soup."

"Good point. It could make a difference about which neighbors we choose to interview."

"Or where Marie was abducted. The route she took could be different from the path the investigator drew in 1968."

"Exactly."

I closed the file. "When do we start talking to witnesses?"

He pointed to the schoolbag. "First, I'll send this item to forensics. They might be able to match the original fingerprints to potential suspects listed in our updated database. They'll try matching any DNA samples they collected from the schoolbag too. Then I'll ask Nadia and Corey to track down the witnesses on file. My goal is to set up interviews for this afternoon, starting with Marie's mother."

Marie Troy's case was now our prime focus, but like Vicky Johnson's case, trying to solve a crime without a body was the hardest thing to do.

3

———————

The red flash from the bankers box containing Marie Troy's case files was a sure sign that she had cried out for my help. From the way Ryan was speeding things along, he had taken an interest in her case too. Luck was with us when Nadia set up our first interview. We would be visiting Mrs. Bernadette Troy, Marie's mother, this afternoon.

Ryan stopped the car at a red light on the drive there. High school students crossed the street in front of us in a flow of blue jeans topped with coats and jackets. Most of the girls and boys carried backpacks in dark or neutral colors. Their cheerful faces lifted my spirits, until I caught a glimpse of a girl in a red coat and remembered the photo of Marie in her red hoodie.

I said to Ryan, "Don't you think it's weird that Marie's schoolbag and lunchbox were found in a garbage pile in the alley? Talk about leaving evidence behind."

"Maybe the abductor panicked. Perps are known to make mistakes with their earlier victims."

"You're saying he could have claimed more than one?"

He shrugged. "Anything's possible."

"Marie was so young. What a horrible loss it must have been for her mother."

Ryan sighed. "I hate speaking with family members and reopening old wounds, especially when we have no answers. We don't even know the motive behind Marie's disappearance."

"A young girl doesn't run away from home and chuck her stuff in the garbage."

"I realize that. What I meant was, she could have been abducted by a wacko for the sick thrill of it. Nothing more. That's for us to find out."

Sandridge Retirement Home overlooked a murky lake that mirrored the sky. Countering the gloomy mood, a gardener tended to bunches of yellow, orange, and pink chrysanthemums bordering the front of the building. Clusters of maple trees in red and gold hues bordered the premises on all sides in a protective hug.

After Ryan and I signed in at the reception desk, an attendant led us to the sitting area. It had two sizable windows and a tall lamp in each corner, but they did nothing to brighten the room. The scent of air fresheners wafted toward us, giving the impression that the premises were clean and well maintained. The gleaming wood floors and dust-free coffee tables confirmed it.

To my right, an elderly woman in a wheelchair sat chatting with a young woman who held her hand. An image of the same young woman crying at a funeral popped into my head. I hated it when these things happened. To clear it from my mind, I gazed out the window at the expansive grounds behind the home dotted with picnic tables.

Footsteps announced another attendant's arrival. "Please follow me." The woman's white sneakers squeaked as she led

Ryan and me down a short corridor. She stopped and tapped on the door to Bernadette Troy's room.

"Come in," a faint voice invited us.

Eighty-three-year-old Mrs. Troy sat in a rocking chair, a quilt over her legs. Her feet barely reached the floor of the modest room she occupied.

Ryan introduced us. "Thanks for meeting with us on such short notice."

"Please, sit down." Mrs. Troy gestured toward folding chairs that had been set up for our visit.

A school photo of Marie sat on an end table next to her. A handful of framed photos of a couple and their three children, probably Bernadette's grandkids, competed for space. A notebook and pen rested nearby.

Despite Mrs. Troy's welcome, her eyes reflected the unrelenting agony of her loss. But I sensed something else: a deep resentment.

She fixed her attention on Ryan. "I understand you're investigating Marie's case."

"That's right." He pulled out his phone to refer to his notes. "We understand you've been through this before with former investigators, but since we're new to the case, we need to confirm the information we have on file."

Mrs. Troy folded her hands. "I'm fine with that."

"Do you remember what Marie was wearing the last time she left for school?"

"Of course I do." Her lips tightened. "A simple white blouse and a navy-blue tunic dress. It was the standard school uniform. Every girl in the primary grades had to wear it or face punishment. Rules were much stricter back then."

"What about a jacket or coat?"

"She wore a red sweatshirt with a hood, or hoodie as you call it today. My ex-husband, Allen, gave it to her. He found it at a girls' athletic club. I can't recall the name. He bought the smallest women's size they had. It was too large for Marie, but how she loved it!" She smiled. "She wore it every day, even if it was warm outside."

I remembered Marie's gold chain in the photo and tested Mrs. Troy's memory. "Did she wear any jewelry?"

She nodded. "Allen gave her a gold ring when she was six years old. It had the letter *M* inscribed inside it. When it grew tight, she wore it on a gold chain I gave her."

"What in particular do you remember about your last morning with Marie?" I asked.

Mrs. Troy released a deep sigh. "Everything. It was the first Monday in April. I'd tied Marie's hair in a ponytail the way she liked to wear it."

Excellent. She confirmed the insight I got when I held the evidence bag containing Marie's hairbrush.

She continued. "They had forecast rain. I handed Marie an umbrella, but she refused it. She said she had too many things to carry already. She had her schoolbag, a lunchbox, and a jar of soup she was to bring to her sick grandmother. She put the hood over her head and left."

"The schoolbag and lunchbox were the items that police investigators discovered after she went missing," Ryan pointed out.

"Yes, they told me about that." Without prompting, Mrs. Troy went on. "I had packed a ham and cheese sandwich, an apple, a tiny box of raisins, and cookies for Marie's lunch. Milk was provided at the school." She looked down and adjusted the quilt over her legs. "Marie always ate her lunch. The police said the untouched food in the lunchbox was proof that she'd gone missing in the morning. The worst part was that the substitute teacher didn't take class attendance that day. I didn't find out Marie was missing until later that afternoon."

I jumped back into the conversation. "Mrs. Troy, let's go back a bit. Marie stopped by her grandmother's home that morning before school. Can you tell us how she got to her grandmother's and how much time she spent there?"

"My mother used to live a few doors down the street from us. She passed away many years ago." She lingered on the memory for a second. "Marie walked along the back alley, like she did when she went to school or visited her grandmother. She didn't stay long. My mother said Marie dropped off the soup and gave her a quick hug before she left."

I recalled a fuzzy detail in the report. "Did your mother say if Marie left by the front door or the back door?"

"Oh, it had to be the back door. It was where the kitchen was in those old houses." At my puzzled look, she added, "It's where family and friends popped in for coffee. The back door was usually unlocked." Her eyes moistened. "I regret having delayed Marie's walk to school that day. If she hadn't stopped at her grandmother's, I could have prevented—"

"You're not to blame," I cut in. "The abductor knew Marie's routine. He had her in his sights the moment she stepped out of your house."

Mrs. Troy's hand flew to her chest. "What? You mean, you know who took her? And no one told me?"

Beside me, Ryan budged restlessly in his chair and threw me a side glance that said, "You're way out of line."

Our interview was far from over, but by Ryan's standards, I'd already trespassed into forbidden territory. It wouldn't have been the first time. I prepared myself for a verbal scolding from him later.

4

———

Marie Troy's abductor had stalked her. Based on my honest perceptions of the evidence in the case, that was the information I'd shared with Marie's mother moments ago.

During our interviews with witnesses, especially family members, I sometimes shared what I saw in my visions. It was my way of answering questions that I sensed they wanted to ask, or in Mrs. Troy's case, to prevent her from feeling guilty about her daughter's disappearance. We didn't have the evidence to support my perception of an abductor in Marie's case, but unfortunately, her mother had accepted my statement as fact.

I'd obviously traumatized her. On top of that, Ryan was upset with me.

To Mrs. Troy, Ryan explained, "It's a theory that Marie's abductor might have planned his move in advance. We have no suspects to date."

"Oh." Her expression crumpled in despair.

"Planned or not, you shouldn't blame yourself for what happened."

She wrung her hands. "I kept hoping Marie was alive all these years. Now I know we'll never find her."

No mother should have to lose a child. The anguish seeping from Mrs. Troy overwhelmed me. Her pain was palpable, like a spirit crushed. I casually slipped a hand in my pocket and clasped the amethyst cluster to calm down.

Ryan acknowledged her sorrow by remaining silent for a few moments, then moved things along. "Mrs. Troy, you said earlier that you found out your daughter was missing later that afternoon. Who informed you?"

Tears welled in her eyes. "Judy White, her friend from school. She dropped by to see how Marie was doing. She was two years older than Marie and sort of a big sister to her. She almost gave me a heart attack when she said Marie didn't meet her that morning. They always walked the rest of the way to school together. I called the school principal immediately, but he was gone for the day. Then I called the police."

"Does Judy still live in the same neighborhood?"

"Oh, I don't know. I haven't seen her since the day Marie..." She blinked. "I guess she felt guilty and wanted to avoid me. A lot of people did...not certain what to say in such a situation. I think it hit Judy hard, poor girl."

Ryan skimmed the notes on his phone. "What can you tell us about your husband, Allen Corbin, and his relationship with your children?"

"My *ex-husband*." She scowled, correcting him. "When we got married, I already had Marie from a previous relationship. Money was tight. We hadn't planned on having more children. Then Tim came along. Accidents happen." She briefly looked away. "But Allen didn't help matters."

"How's that?"

"Tim had a stuttering problem, and Allen had no patience for it. He ignored Tim. The poor kid would do things to please him, but he'd ignore him. Tim would play alone. He amused himself by collecting playing cards, colorful stones from the backyard, stamps from envelopes...small things." She stiffened. "What I hated the most about Allen was that he made his preference for Marie so obvious. He drove her to school when he wasn't away on business. He often gave her gifts."

"Daddy's little girl."

"That's for sure." Mrs. Troy let out a weary sigh. "Allen took Marie to the girls' swim club the summer before she...." She choked on the words, then went on. "Parents complained that he'd touched their young daughters, that he was a dirty old man, if you know what I mean. Allen denied it, but I had a very bad feeling about it."

"Is that why your marriage broke up?"

"No, it was much more personal than that. I found out he was sleeping around." Her nose crinkled in disgust. "I kicked him out. I told him not to come back, that he'd never see the kids again. We had an awful argument. Tim was there."

Ryan and I said nothing.

Mrs. Troy's focus shifted to the framed photos on the end table, as if she were about to dredge up another painful memory. Instead, she reached for a photo tucked under the notebook. "After the officer called to set up our meeting, I dug this photo out of an old album." She handed it to Ryan. "She was one of the reasons I kicked Allen out. I kept it as a reminder of how much he'd hurt me."

It was a creased Polaroid photo of a young preteen girl. Dressed in her underwear, she sat coyly on a bed, a clock on the bedside table beside her. On the back of the photo and scribbled in childlike handwriting was the note, *Thanks for tonight, from your Toronto love, Debbie.* A date was scrawled underneath.

"Looks can be deceiving," Ryan said, "but this girl doesn't seem to be more than twelve years old."

"A child," Mrs. Troy said, pursing her lips.

"How did you get this?"

"Months after I threw Allen out, he paid me an unexpected visit. It was the day Marie went missing. He had a birthday gift for her. A Barbie doll. It was all the rage back then. While Allen used the bathroom, Tim searched the pockets of his jacket as usual and found the picture. I kept it and showed it to my lawyer."

"Did Allen find out?"

"You bet. He signed the divorce papers real fast." She laughed.

Ryan tapped the photo. "Can we borrow this?"

"Keep it," Mrs. Troy said. "It's no good to me anymore."

He tucked it in his pocket and returned to a previous subject. "What time did Allen arrive at your home that morning?"

She hesitated. "Um...I'm not sure. Later in the morning, for sure. Marie had already left for school."

He circled back to an earlier topic. "Mrs. Troy, you mentioned that Marie often walked along the alley. Aside from your mother, did she visit or see anyone else along that path? Her friends, for example?"

"Marie had lots of friends at school," she said, "but none of them lived within walking distance from us." She paused. "Oh...she did play with the neighbor's dog whenever he let her."

"Which neighbor?

"His name was Gaston Belair."

I'd seen the name in Marie's file. Gaston was one of the people investigators had interviewed. If Ryan recalled the name, he showed no signs of it. Then again, it was in his nature to be discreet when gathering evidence.

"What can you tell us about him?" Ryan asked her.

"He was about eighteen years old at the time," Mrs. Troy said. "When his parents died in an accident years later, he inherited their triplex a few doors over. He owned a dog. I don't know the breed, but it wasn't a big dog. The first time it wandered into our backyard, Marie wanted to keep it. I knew it belonged to someone because it had a collar with an ID tag.

After Marie returned the dog to Gaston, he let her play with it in his backyard now and then."

Ryan entered a note on his phone. "What kind of work did Gaston do?"

"He worked in construction but did repairs and other chores for people in the neighborhood. He was pretty good at it too." She paused, remembering. "He kept to himself and wasn't very sociable. After he got to know me better, he opened up and told me how his parents had beat him as a child. Poor boy."

"Where's Gaston now?"

"I have no idea. He moved away a couple of years ago, around the same time Tim was helping me relocate to this retirement home. From what my friends tell me, Gaston hasn't kept up with repairs on the three-story house. He rented it out for a while, then put it up for sale but hasn't sold it." She surveyed the room. "I can't believe I've been here for two years already. I suffered from a painful back and needed more help to get around than I thought. Thank goodness for Tim."

"How can we reach Tim?"

Mrs. Troy scribbled Tim's phone number and home address on a paper and handed it to him. "I'm so lucky to have three wonderful grandchildren who visit me every week or so." She pointed to the photos on the table and smiled. "Children are so precious."

"Yes, they are," I said. "Mrs. Troy, do you know anyone who might have wanted to harm Marie? Anyone who took an unusual interest in children?"

"Funny you should mention that. There was a junk collector who pushed a cart through the alley every week. He'd rummage through the trash for items like empty glass bottles, metal cans, and old clothes. They weren't of value to anyone else, but I imagine he sold them for a living. Anyway, he always brought his dog along. Marie loved animals, so she and her little friends would flock to him. The older kids were another story. They teased the poor man. They'd shout, 'Hobo, full of fleas' at him, over and over."

"Did he ever react to their teasing?"

Mrs. Troy's eyes went wide. "I'll say. One day I saw him through my kitchen window. He chased the kids after they'd pestered him. Marie happened to be standing nearby. The kids scattered, but the junk collector chased Marie into our backyard. She was screaming, yelling 'Mommy.' I ran out and accused him of scaring the children. He laughed and walked off. I didn't have to warn Marie to stay away from him. She was scared enough. He stopped passing by weeks later. Maybe he found a better alley."

My apprehension grew. "Did you report him to the police?"

"Yes, after Marie went missing."

"What did they do?"

"Nothing. They ignored me when I said he might be involved."

Ryan rejoined the conversation. "Do you know the junk collector's name?"

"No," Mrs. Troy said.

"Any other incidents with neighbors?"

She shook her head. "With housework, a young child, and starting a new job after I threw Allen out, I was too busy to socialize. Oh, he'd give me money for Tim's clothes and stuff, but after he remarried, the money stopped coming."

Ryan asked one last question. "Mrs. Troy, do we have your permission to create a video about Marie and air it on TV? Add it to a missing persons show to appeal for help from the public?"

"Of course," she said. "I'm so grateful that the police are finally listening to me. I was shocked that they didn't come back to see me or let me know what was happening. It was if they didn't care about my daughter. I've been angry for so many years." She took out a tissue and dabbed at her eyes. "But now you're here."

He leaned forward. "I'm sorry you had to wait this long. We'll be doing everything possible to solve Marie's case. It's never too late to serve justice."

She stiffened. "Then you might want to talk to Allen."

"Why?"

"He hated me for kicking him out. My greatest fear is that Marie might have been an innocent victim of his twisted desires."

"In what way?" Ryan asked.

"His fondness for young girls, if you know what I mean." She blinked hard, as if to wipe out an image. "I think he kidnapped Marie to get back at me. He knew how much it would hurt me." She tightened her hold on the quilt.

"Did you mention your suspicions to police investigators?"

"Yes, but they said they needed proof. They basically dismissed me."

~

After Ryan and I left the retirement home, relief washed over me like a warm bath. I'd sensed the range of Mrs. Troy's emotions in that isolated room: from sadness to regret, from despair to hope, from anger to retribution. Gulping a breath of fresh air helped to remove the negativity.

As we drove out of the parking lot, Ryan asked me, "So? What do you think?"

He often asked about my impressions after an interview. It was a sign he appreciated my input. This time, it didn't come with a reproach. "What? No lecture for what I said to Mrs. Troy about the abductor?"

"I realize you meant well, Amber, but your claim devastated her. This is police business, so try to keep your perceptions for our private discussions. Okay?" He steered the car into the passing lane.

"Okay." I expected worse. Was he mellowing because of our

personal relationship? "To answer your question, Mrs. Troy's allegation about her ex-husband didn't surprise me. She suspects he abducted Marie to retaliate against her. We need to take a closer look at Allen Corbin."

He turned right at the intersection. "About Allen's history... What passed for gossip decades ago wouldn't pass the smell test today. A recently divorced man suspected of assaulting young girls, taking a photo of a preteen girl in her underwear... He sounds like a possible pedophile to me."

"But you said nothing criminal showed up for him in the database."

"It doesn't mean anything. These guys know how to hide their tracks. I'll ask Corey to locate Allen's recent address. We need to talk to him."

"What about Gaston, the neighbor with the dog? There was a time lapse not accounted for in his work schedule the morning Marie went missing."

"Right. He's definitely a person of interest. So is the junk collector, if we can find him."

5

Nadia designed a page for Marie Troy on the police website the next morning. She posted file photos of the missing girl at eight years old, her physical description, and what she was wearing the day she disappeared. The site included a dedicated phone number to the Info-Crime line at the unit.

"Arrange for an illustrator to create progression sketches of Marie periodically through the years," Ryan said to Nadia. "If she's alive, and there's the slightest hope that someone might have recognized her at a later stage of her life, it would be a bonus." To Corey, he said, "Run a criminal check on Gaston Belair. Let me know what you find."

Ryan and I planned to work rotating shifts with Nadia and Corey to handle incoming calls after the site was up and running. A dispatcher from homicide would cover the night shift. When we considered the helpful calls we'd received regarding other cold cases, we were counting once again on the public to provide us with anonymous tips.

Yet doubts filtered my mind. Would anyone call the police with information about Marie Troy decades later? Would anyone be brave enough to come forward? I shared my qualms with Ryan.

"That's why we're heading out to do the legwork now." He grabbed his jacket. "You ready?"

"What legwork?"

"You'll see."

And I did. Hours later, after knocking on dozens of doors and interviewing residents in a three-block radius from Marie Troy's former home, we realized dismal results: no leads. While many of the former occupants had moved away or were deceased, a handful of current residents we interviewed were able to give us those names. Corey ran all the names we'd gathered through the criminal database, but to our disappointment, he reported no hits.

Ryan studied the reports Corey had handed him. "What do you think, Amber? Should we pick another case?"

"No way," I said, wondering if he were testing me. "This case called out to me. I'm determined to see it through to the end."

Our attention was diverted that afternoon when Ryan and I had an impromptu meeting with Detective Sergeant Matt Gallo. Since he was new to the unit, he was eager to get our feedback about the case he was working on. When Lieutenant Payton first mentioned he wanted to add one more investigator to our team, Ryan had suggested Matt. They'd worked on homicide cases together, so Ryan believed his experience would benefit the unit.

I'd had limited interaction with Matt since his arrival a week ago. I wanted to approach him with an open mind, but I'd already sensed something about him that I didn't like. For the sake of the unit, I tried to move past it. After all, the lieutenant expected nothing less than teamwork.

Enthusiasm spread across Matt's round face as he prepared to update us on Louise Lavoie's cold case. Standing by a section of the crazy wall dedicated to his case, he opened a manila file. "Let me begin with the history. Ten-year-old Louise Lavoie vanished one night in 1967. She had a disorder called somnambulism, or sleepwalking, as we know it. She'd wake up during the night and walk out the door. Then she'd go down the exterior stairs leading from the family's second-story apartment."

"Wow, that's scary," I said.

Matt went on. "Her parents were terrified that she might slip and fall down the stairs, especially in the winter when the stairs were icy. Then she'd stroll along the street in the middle of the night. Sometimes a neighbor would alert the family, but most often, her parents would discover she was missing and go look for her."

I leaned forward in my chair. "Had her parents locked the doors to prevent her from leaving?"

"Yes, according to their statements. In fact, they were surprised she managed to undo the double bolt on the front door. She was just a wisp of a kid." He pointed toward the crazy wall where he'd pinned the photo of a tiny girl with brown eyes and dark curly hair." Luckily, one of her parents found her every time and guided her back home. Except for the last time." He grimaced.

"You said she went missing in 1967," Ryan said. "Amber and I are working on another case involving an eight-year-old girl named Marie Troy. She vanished in April of the following year." He pointed to details of Marie's case he'd written on an adjacent section of the crazy wall.

"Yes, I know," Matt said. "I reviewed those notes earlier. Louise Lavoie in October 1967, six months before Marie Troy. And on Halloween night. Pretty wild, eh?"

"Maybe Louise was a test run for the abductor," I said.

"Not a bad theory," Matt said, staring at me longer than necessary. "I'd sure hate for that to happen to any of my kids."

"How old are your kids?"

"My girls are eight and ten."

"Matt," Ryan interrupted, "what else have you got?"

"More interesting stuff. It seemed like a coincidence at first, but there's a distinct pattern here. When I ran a check on the database, I discovered that a rash of child abductions had occurred in the same narrow geographical area."

"The black pins I put on the map represent those cases," Ryan pointed out.

"Yes, I saw that. What I'm getting at is this. Isn't it weird that investigators didn't see a trend back then or make the connection between all those cases?"

"It was due to a lack of resources or time," Ryan said. "What's the proximity of our two case victims?"

"The girls lived six blocks apart."

"Show me on the crazy wall."

Matt stuck two red pins on the board to mark the girls' residential locations.

Ryan leaned forward. "As far as geographic profiling goes, the similar time period and the proximity of the victims could point to the same abductor. Most likely, he lived or frequented the same area. What about the schools the girls attended?"

Matt shook his head. "They didn't go to the same school."

"Any statements from witnesses regarding the night of Louise's disappearance?"

"None so far. Her sister is the only living relative. She was six years old and, like her parents, she was asleep when Louise left the house. No one heard or saw a thing until they discovered she was missing the next morning."

"Any other leads?"

Matt closed the file and sat down at his desk. "Investigators went door to door the next day but got nothing. No leads. No body. No evidence."

Ryan leaned back in his chair and clasped his hands behind his head, thinking. "We have a similar MO in both cases. The same perp might have kidnapped Louise that night, then got bolder months later and took Marie off the street in broad daylight. He had to be familiar with the children's routines and how to entice them so as not to arouse suspicion."

"What was Louise wearing that night?" I asked.

"A long white nightgown. Which reminds me." Matt flipped through the file. "Residents who'd seen her walking at night told investigators she looked like a sleeping beauty floating along the sidewalk. In fact, they started to call her by that name."

I drew in a quick breath. "Another fairy-tale implication. It can't be a coincidence." I glanced at Ryan for a sign that he agreed.

He shrugged. "Anything's possible."

Matt's lips curled up in a smile. "Oh, I get it. It's like the red hoodie case you're working on: 'Little Red Riding Hood.' It's a valid reason to suspect the same perp is connected to both cases."

Ryan's phone rang and he took the call. His conversation sounded personal, so he retreated to a corner of the room.

I stood up. "I need a cup of coffee."

"I'll join you." Matt followed me to the kitchen.

I was about to reach for a cup when Matt beat me to it. He pulled out two cups and filled them, then handed me one. "So tell me, Amber. What do you do for fun? A beautiful girl like you must have lots of guys chasing her in bars."

I was annoyed that this forty-something man would be so inquisitive about my private life. "My weekends are generally quiet."

"You could have fooled me." He stepped closer to me, his stomach protruding from his unbuttoned jacket. "We can change that." He ran a finger along my arm.

"I have a boyfriend," I blurted, taking a step back, spilling coffee on the floor and down the front of my shirt. "Oh no!"

Matt grabbed a paper towel from the dispenser and moved toward me, aiming for my shirt.

"No!" I said.

Ryan entered the kitchen and stopped, his eyes flitting from me to Matt. "What the hell is going on here?"

I placed my cup on the counter and took the paper towel from Matt. "Nothing that I can't handle." I dabbed at my shirt, then wiped the spill on the floor.

"Nothing," Matt echoed and hurried out.

Since Ryan had recommended Matt for the job, I didn't want to make a big deal out of the incident. I felt confident that I'd sent Matt a clear message anyway. He wouldn't flirt with me again.

I picked up my coffee cup. "That phone call you got, Ryan. Is everything okay?"

"The retirement home called about my mother. I need to talk to her about something."

When he said nothing more about it, I let it go. He needed time to work out whatever was going on with his mother.

After we returned to our desks, Ryan picked up the discussion with our coworker about the case he was investigating. "Matt, did the evidence box for Louise Lavoie contain any of her personal belongings?"

"Not a damn thing." Matt tapped the bankers box with his pen. "I knew we needed something for DNA purposes if we ever nabbed a suspect, so I called her sister. I asked her for a personal item that had belonged to Louise, like clothing or a toy. She said she'd get back to me." He leaned forward in his chair. "What's next?"

"Here's the thing," Ryan said. "If people happened to look out their window the night Louise vanished, they might not have realized they'd witnessed a crime. You need to interview the neighbors on her street. Expand your search radius to three blocks. Try to track down the names of residents who might have relocated from there."

Matt gaped at him. "You can't be serious."

"I am."

He let out a low whistle. "For Pete's sake, Ryan, that's a lot of legwork, and it was such a long time ago."

"Amber and I just finished our sprint in Marie Troy's area.

You need to cover all bases, like you did in homicide. People gossip. They might have heard something about that night from other neighbors who were too afraid to talk to police."

Matt folded his arms. "You said working in this unit would be a lot easier than homicide."

"Not quite. I said working on cold cases would be easier on crisis response."

Matt grumbled, "Anything else?"

"After you collect the witness names, ask Corey to run them through the database for background checks."

"Fine." Matt stood up and tucked his phone in his jacket. "See you guys later." He glanced at me and acted as if nothing had happened between us earlier.

All the better. I didn't need more drama in my life. The upcoming interviews with other witnesses in Marie Troy's case were sure to provide an ample supply of it.

6

Corey smiled with confidence as he handed Ryan a report. "Sergeant Baxter, I searched the local and national police databases and came up with this info in Marie Troy's case so far. I'm also close to confirming a fixed address for one of your persons of interest."

"Thanks, Corey," Ryan said. "Good job."

Corey gave him a nod and strutted back to his desk.

Ryan scanned the details. "Amber, listen to this. Allen Troy is currently in the hospital. No condition given." He read on. "Gaston Belair racked up three speeding tickets and demerit points in the last two years. The address on record for him is unconfirmed, though Corey is still checking it out like he said. If we can talk to these guys, it could offer more leads, or at least narrow down our suspect list."

"Gaston is in his seventies, and Allen is in his eighties," I said. "If they had something to do with Louise's kidnapping and eluded police all these years, why do you think they would confess to it today?"

"If they managed to stay off the police radar for more

serious crimes, it doesn't mean anything. Perps get away with murder. The cold cases alone are proof of it."

"I understand, but it sounds as if you're counting on someone to confess."

"It's called contrition," Ryan said. "Sometimes perps don't get a chance to make up for their crimes. They take the opportunity to do it in their old age. It's their way of seeking absolution for their sins." He stood up, adjusted his tie, and slipped into his jacket.

"Where are you going?"

"*We* are going to visit our next witness: Allen Corbin."

I grabbed my handbag and followed him out.

As we crossed the parking lot to the car, I made my position clear to Ryan. "I've been having second thoughts about Allen Corbin. I believe Mrs. Troy was exaggerating when she hinted that he kidnapped her daughter. Allen has no record of criminal offenses, and he has an alibi for that day. Previous investigators confirmed he was away on business in Toronto."

"Here's the thing," he said, buckling up. "Mrs. Troy said Allen arrived after Marie had left for school. My theory is that he might have driven during the night and reached Montreal long before popping in to see her. Dropping off a birthday gift could have been a cover-up."

"Or he simply popped in to deliver the birthday gift."

He chuckled. "Playing the devil's advocate, are we?" He drove out of the parking lot and merged into traffic.

"Sort of. Someone has to keep you on your toes." I smiled.

"Then I'm glad it's you." Ryan reached over and squeezed my hand. "Anyway, it's about a six-hour drive from Toronto to Montreal. If Allen has solid proof of his whereabouts, it'll remove him from the time frame of Marie's disappearance, and we can eliminate him as a suspect."

"Proof? As in receipts?"

"Yes."

"We're talking decades ago. Digital receipts didn't exist back then. What if he didn't keep his receipts? I mean, who would keep them that long?"

"Then he has a problem."

Even though I hadn't met Allen, I was already feeling sorry for him.

~

We were met with a shocking revelation upon our arrival at the Royal Victoria Hospital. Allen Corbin had suffered a heart attack and was recovering in the intensive care unit. The nurse cautioned us that our visit was limited to five minutes.

Allen's sparse blond-gray hair blended into an ashen complexion while pain clouded intense blue eyes that had seen better days. Medical equipment hooked up to his slender body monitored his vital signs, sending out subtle, periodic beeps like seconds on a clock. His apparent struggle to breathe left no doubt that his health was failing.

Ryan introduced us. "Mr. Corbin, we're currently reviewing Marie Troy's disappearance in 1968. Can you tell us where you were the day she was reported missing?"

"I was away on business in Toronto," Allen replied.

"Our records indicate you were in Montreal that morning."

"Oh...right." He took a gulp of air. "I drove back to Montreal during the night...got there in the morning."

"It's a six-hour drive. Did you stop along the way?"

Allen squinted at the ceiling. "Yes. I had a bite to eat at an all-night diner."

"Do you have any proof? A receipt from the diner?"

"The police asked me the same question. I paid in cash and got a receipt, but I couldn't find it later. Investigators stopped bothering me about it eventually." He inhaled deeply. "I guess they spent their days trying to find Marie instead."

Ryan sped up his line of questioning. "What time did you arrive in Montreal?"

"I can't remember exactly," Allen said. "Early in the morning. It was Marie's birthday. I'd bought her a Barbie doll, so I went to see her." He breathed deeply. "Bernadette—her mother—told me she'd already left for school."

Ryan persisted. "What time was that?"

"What difference does it make?" As he stared at Ryan, his expression abruptly changed from annoyance to surprise. "You think I kidnapped Marie? Is this why you're here?"

Ryan kept his gaze on Allen and remained quiet.

"I'd never hurt Marie. I loved her!" He coughed, then began to pant. "When I learned about her abduction...I couldn't believe it...I was horrified."

As I adjusted my shoulder bag, my hand accidentally brushed the bed. A black haze suddenly formed around Allen, then evaporated when I took a step back.

What was that black haze? I'd never experienced anything like it before. Was something wrong with me? I reached into my jacket, gripping the amethyst crystal for composure.

Ryan interrupted my thoughts. "Mr. Corbin, I understand that you cheated on your first wife."

"Yes." Allen's breathing grew raspy. "Bernadette didn't deserve the rotten way I treated her. She kicked me out...kept me away from the kids."

"So you got even by taking Marie from her."

"You're wrong." Allen's eyes watered. "I loved those kids. I wished I'd been a better father to them. God punished me for my negligence."

"What do you mean?"

"My second marriage...my wife couldn't have children."

I said to him, "Mr. Corbin, you have a son. Tim."

He blinked. "I called him years ago...kept in touch with him. I needed to make it up to him...all those times I mistreated him..." He wheezed. "I'm so sorry for what I did...to those children..."

"Which children?" I asked.

Allen clutched his throat and gasped for air.

His patient monitor sounded an alarm.

A nurse rushed in and placed an oxygen mask over his nose and mouth. She adjusted a line, silencing the alarm, then turned to us. "You'll have to leave now. Your visiting time is over."

~

I'd witnessed a man who was most likely on his deathbed. It was unnerving. Even more so was the black haze I'd seen around him. Did I have a problem with my vision, or was I starting to see things that weren't there? Whatever it was, I couldn't wait to get outdoors and take in the fresh air.

As we walked to the parking lot, Ryan said to me. "What do you make of our visit with Allen?"

"It was strange the way he referred to mistreating children," I said. "Whose children? His children?"

"Yeah, that was weird."

"I sensed genuine regret from him, though."

"It doesn't mean anything." Ryan slid in behind the wheel. "He can't prove his alibi. His uncertainty about the time of his arrival in Montreal places him within the narrow period that Marie went missing."

His reply stunned me. "So you've already determined he's guilty?"

"Not at all. I'm trying to keep an open mind."

I was wondering if I was losing mine. I remained quiet.

"What aren't you telling me, Amber?" He gave me a quick glance. "Did you get any insights back there?"

Talk about being in sync. Although I was certain it would sound crazy, I told him about the black haze I'd seen around Allen.

Ryan frowned. "What does it mean?"

"I don't know, but I'm going to find out."

~

I called Aunt Elaine that evening to get her clarification of the black haze around Allen.

"It's dead energy, dear," she said, gentleness filtering through her voice. "It happens when people go through a spiritual or emotional growth phase. When the soul is ready to release the energy, it appears like tiny particles in a dark mist or smoke."

"Dead energy? Does it mean the person is dying?"

"Not necessarily, though the man's poor health doesn't sound promising. Otherwise, what you perceived is a positive sign."

"In what way?"

"Your ability to see these things reinforces your psychic gift, dear. Accept your perceptions with an objective mind, and move on from there. Otherwise, you'll wear yourself out with worry."

I thanked her for the advice and promised to visit with her and Uncle Ted soon.

"Accept your perceptions with an objective mind," my aunt had said. As a psychic *and* an empath, staying detached when reviewing criminal evidence was my ultimate challenge. Despite the drawback, I was prepared. Investigating a little girl's disappearance would strengthen my determination to confront that challenge head-on.

7

——————

My phone rang minutes after I arrived at my desk the next morning. I smiled when I saw Nicole Latour's name displayed. A close friend since our university days, Nicole was a schoolteacher who lived in an apartment within walking distance of my house.

"Hi, Amber. It's been ages since we last got together. I'm calling you before you make other plans for the weekend." Her bubbly voice rang with the promise of fun and laughter.

"What do you have in mind?" I swiveled in my chair and huddled behind my computer screen.

"Are you free this Sunday afternoon?"

"Sunday afternoon? Yes."

"Are you sure I won't be taking you away from that handsome man in your life? Is he hanging around your desk right now?"

I laughed. "Yes and yes."

"*Fantastique!*" Nicole's French-Canadian vocabulary slipped into the conversation as it often did. "You can come over to my place. Bring potato chips. I have lots of everything else." She giggled.

"Sounds good. See you then."

Ryan poked his head around his computer. "That was your friend, Nicole. Right?"

"Yes. We're having our usual get-together this weekend."

His jaw dropped. "*All* weekend?"

Did I detect a hint of jealousy? He was probably worried that I'd canceled our plans for Saturday night. Having dinner and spending an evening together once a week was something we enjoyed, whether it was at his place or mine.

I looked around. Matt was out interviewing witnesses. Nadia and Corey were busy doing computer work.

"It's been weeks since Nicole and I got together," I whispered, teasing him. "We have to catch up."

"I see," Ryan said, disappointment in his voice.

"On Sunday afternoon."

Relief swept over his face. "Oh! That's good." A ping on his phone drew his attention. After he checked the message, he stood up and put on his jacket. "Let's go. We have another witness to interview in Marie Troy's case."

"Who?"

"Tim Corbin. He agreed to meet with us."

A short drive across the Champlain Bridge brought us to Candiac, an off-island suburb of Montreal located on the south shore of the Saint Lawrence River. Gray clouds lingered overhead and cast a disquieting ambiance over our impending interview.

Or was I sensing the ominous mood from something else? The witnesses we interviewed released emotions that were unpredictable, if not impossible, to prepare for. Was I picking up Tim's feelings?

We parked in the driveway of a modest split-level bungalow and stepped out. A gust of wind blew the scent of freshly cut grass in our direction. As we walked along a stone path to the house, Ryan gave me a *Hope this turns out to be a valuable interview* look before he rang the bell.

A slim man with the same straight blond hair and blue eyes as Allen Corbin opened the front door. Tim was without a doubt his father's son. Although he was almost sixty, he gave the impression he was much younger. His boyish smile was a definite factor.

As we settled in the living room, I spotted the photos of Tim's children on the mantel above the fireplace. Although nothing would replace the loss of Marie, this generation of Mrs. Troy's family had most likely helped to ease the burden.

Tim rested his hands on the armchair across from us. "The officer from your police unit said you wanted to talk to me about Marie."

"That's right," Ryan said. "We understand you were a young boy back then, but can you tell us what you remember about the day Marie disappeared?"

"I was only four years old. My parents would be in a better position to answer your questions."

"We've already met with your mother. We visited your father this morning at the hospital. He told us he's kept in touch with you."

"Yeah, he called me the other day and told me he was pretty sick. I went to see him in the hospital. I hope he pulls through."

Ryan held back from mentioning that we were asked to leave due to Allen's deteriorating condition. "How would you describe your relationship with your father?"

"Excellent. My kids are finally getting to know their grandfather after all these years." He smiled. "I'm grateful for that, but I wish he would have reached out to us sooner."

"Why do you think he waited so long?"

Tim's shoulders slumped. "Because he liked Marie b-b-better. He always ignored me. Even when I tried so hard to b-b-be really g-g-good."

I was stunned at the way he hastily relapsed into stuttering when he spoke about how his father had snubbed him as a child. Even after all these years, his sadness was so intense that I could feel it.

Tim crossed his arms. "As a kid, I couldn't understand why my father had no time for me. I felt left out. So I'd steal b-b-bits of his love now and then."

"Steal?" I repeated. "What do you mean?"

He lowered his eyes, as if he was embarrassed about his disclosure. "I'd take little things that he stashed in his suit pockets when he returned from b-b-business trips. Coins, notes, receipts. Small stuff with numbers on them. I'd stash them away like mementos."

"They reminded you of your father," I said.

"Yes." Tim breathed deeply and placed his hands in his lap, relaxing. He spoke slowly without stuttering. "In spite of his absence, I managed to make a life for myself. After I finished high school, I worked during the day and took speech therapy classes at night." He paused to take another deep breath. "I took a business course. I liked numbers and worked as an accountant until I retired last year. People finally respected and valued me. I'm proud of what I accomplished. When my father asked for my forgiveness, I gave it to him."

"It sounds as if you've reconciled with your father," Ryan said. "That's why the next question might offend you, but I need to ask for investigative purposes. Did your father ever physically abuse you or Marie?"

Tim jerked upright. "No! My mother wouldn't have allowed it."

"How do you know that?"

"Because he cheated on her and she didn't accept that. She'd do anything to protect us. The day she threw him out of the house, he threatened that he'd take Marie and me away from her. I heard him. My mother was so scared. She cried for days afterward."

Ryan guided the conversation to the next topic. "As a young boy back then, do you remember anything about your neighbors? Someone who took a special interest in Marie or other young children?"

"If you mean in a weird way, not really," Tim said. "After Marie went missing, I wasn't allowed to play outside, except in the backyard. Apart from family and friends who visited, the only adult I saw was the man who did repair jobs for us. Gaston Belair. He came to the house to fix things a few times. I don't remember what he looks like. I do remember that he was quiet and rarely spoke, though."

"Do you know a relative or friend of the family who might have wanted to harm Marie?"

"No. And that includes my father. He has regrets about the way he treated me, but he's not a bad person."

"So you don't think he was capable of kidnapping or harming Marie?"

"No way," Tim said, emphasizing his conviction. "She meant the world to him. My mother is convinced that he took Marie out of revenge. I don't believe it for a second."

What a contrast! Unlike his mother, Tim had not only forgiven his father, but now he was also defending him.

Ryan checked his notes. "Your father said he was traveling the day Marie vanished. He stopped at a diner and maybe made another stop for gas, but he hasn't been able to provide receipts."

"How could he? They didn't have digital records in those days."

"You're right, but they issued cash register or handwritten receipts. In any case, your father hasn't been able to prove his alibi."

"That's unfortunate. It might not matter at this point...my father having receipts, I mean." Tim looked away.

"Why not?"

Tim blinked back the tears. "I spoke with his doctors. They

said his prognosis was poor, that he doesn't have long to live. It could be days. I'm hopeful, though."

His disclosure weighed heavily on me. It signaled not only an impending personal loss for Tim but also an obstacle in solving Marie's case.

What if Allen died before we completed our investigation? If he were indeed Marie's abductor, it meant we'd have no way of proving it, and the case would remain as cold as ever.

8

———————

Ryan and I updated the crazy wall with details from our witness interviews in Marie Troy's case. A question mark below the photo of Allen Corbin, one of our persons of interest, was a reminder of the limited progress we'd made in closing in on the real perpetrator. We needed to locate and interview other persons of interest, like Gaston Belair and the garbage collector who remained anonymous so far. We added question marks under their name cards too.

A forensic analysis of samples from Marie Troy's schoolbag revealed the DNA was so degraded that it provided no clues. While I continued to experience feelings of dread whenever I held the vintage red and black plaid item by its handle, I couldn't tap into the aggressor's identity or perceive more of his physical traits beyond an unshaven face.

Frustration set in. We needed to solve Marie's case more than anything. As the lieutenant reminded us on frequent occasions, our jobs depended on it.

Ryan tried to reassure me after I'd tried to get a more significant impression from the schoolbag and failed again. "It's okay.

We have other people to interview. Something's bound to pop up."

The confidence in his voice was encouraging. He was right. We were only days into investigating Marie's case. More evidence was bound to surface. We couldn't let desperation affect our rational thinking.

"Hey, guys." Matt strolled in with a confident air, his portfolio in one hand and a bag in the other. "I got new evidence for Louise Lavoie's case. Her sister gave me this Snoopy toy." He set his portfolio down, then held the evidence bag up for us to see.

Like Snoopy in the cast of *Peanuts*, the plush toy had a black nose, black eyes, and black floppy ears. A short red shirt hung open over a white body that had yellowed with age, but the overall ragged appearance of the toy was proof that it had been loved.

"Her sister told me Louise loved this toy above all others," Matt said, confirming my belief. "She had it with her the night she went out walking in her sleep but dropped it on the street."

Ryan gave him a thumbs-up. "Good work. We'll send it out for DNA analysis. The perp who kidnapped her might have touched it."

Matt dropped the bag on Ryan's desk and moved to the crazy wall. He added details in the section for Louise Lavoie.

I caught Ryan's subtle nod toward the Snoopy toy. I nodded back. I was as eager as he was to garner insights from it, but we'd have to wait until later when no one was around. I'd already attracted too much curiosity from colleagues after reacting to insights from evidence.

"Guys," Matt called out. "Come over to the crazy wall. I want to show you something." After we joined him, he pointed to the city map where pins marked out a six-block radius. "You see this area? We already know that other young girls went missing here in the 1960s, including Marie and Louise. What's wild is that all of a sudden, the kidnappings stopped."

"One explanation is that the perp could have moved away," Ryan said. "Or died."

"You think he's dead?" Matt sounded skeptical. "I'm not so sure. We learned from experience how serial killers manage to hide their tracks." He turned to me with a penetrating stare. "What do you think, Amber?"

I couldn't very well come out and say I'd had an insight that indicated Marie's abductor was alive. "I-I don't know."

"You must have an idea. Don't you have a background in criminology or something?"

I was astounded. He was questioning my qualifications. "Well, I studied—"

"Matt, what are you getting at?" Ryan's voice resonated with impatience.

Matt raised his arms. "Hey, I just want to establish that we're all on the same footing here. You and I have experience in criminal investigation. What's Amber's background? I mean, she is kind of young."

"Age means nothing. Amber came highly recommended for her analytical work in criminology."

I almost burst out laughing at Ryan's attempt to describe my psychic abilities in scientific terms.

Ryan gestured toward the crazy wall. "You brought us over here to discuss the cases. Get to the point, Matt."

Matt relented. "Fine. My point is, seeing as our cases have overlapping territory and most serial killers hunt close to home, we might be looking for the same perp."

"We already discussed the possibility. So?"

"If he's still alive, one of your persons of interest might be connected to my case. How about I interview them?"

"Not the best idea, Matt."

"Why not?"

"Amber and I have already set up meetings with them. We need to clear potential suspects before you jump in."

Matt grimaced in exasperation. "But I have no other leads."

"Sorry, Matt." Ryan's tone was firm. "You'll have to wait. The last thing we want to do is scare our potential perps by interviewing them about one criminal case after another. They'd go into hiding."

Matt raised his voice. "That's not fair, Ryan. I thought we'd be working these cases together." He eyed me with a hint of contempt, as if I were impeding his teamwork.

"We *are* working together," Ryan said. "Our case notes are up on the crazy wall next to yours. Of course, we need to update them because things are moving quickly."

Was Ryan serious about sharing our case notes with Matt? I'd recorded my psychic insights in there!

Ryan went on. "As far as interviewing our persons of interest, we can't afford to have any of them disappear. Like I said, we need to clear other suspects first."

Matt grit his jaw, holding back a retort. "Fine. Have it your way. I'm off to interview people." He picked up his portfolio and noisily stormed past Nadia and Corey on his way out.

As we returned to our desks, I whispered to Ryan, "Matt knows you're leading this group. Yet he doesn't take orders well, does he?"

He reached for the evidence bag that Matt had abandoned, then pulled up a chair next to me. "It's his weak spot," he said, keeping his voice low. "Otherwise, he's a capable investigator."

"He questioned my ability to do the job. How do you expect me to work with him?"

"Ignore him. He's frustrated that he hasn't come up with anything substantial in Louise Lavoie's case so far. We can help him. Do you have a moment to...you know." He held out the Snoopy toy to me.

I felt the softness of the plush toy through the evidence bag. On closer examination, I noticed that one of the three tiny buttons on Snoopy's red shirt was coming loose. All of a sudden, I bent over, struggling for air. I dropped the evidence bag as I struggled to turn off my empathic gift.

"Amber!" Ryan placed a hand on my back, fear threading in his voice. "Amber, what's the matter?"

I straightened up and raised a hand to signal I was okay. My breathing slowly returned to normal. "I got a terrible sense of choking in a dark place."

"Anything else?"

"No."

Unnoticed, Nadia had hurried up to us. She stood by my desk, staring curiously at me. "Are you feeling dizzy again, Amber? You look pale."

"Uh...yes." I managed a brief smile. "It'll pass."

Doubt flickered in her eyes before she handed me a file. "Here's the info you wanted on the two women for the Marie Troy case."

"Did you have any trouble locating them?"

Nadia shook her head, causing her long dark curls to bounce off her shoulders. "There were dozens of women with the name Judy White living in Montreal, but I managed to find her on LinkedIn. No problem finding Sarina Bruno either."

"Thanks."

She pointed to a note attached to one of the files. "I've set up interviews with both women this afternoon. I'm still tracking down the other names you gave me. I'll let you know if I find anything else." She strolled back to her desk, her shoulders squared in a self-assured manner.

"That was close," I whispered to Ryan.

"Yeah. It might be a better idea to do your psychic thing somewhere else. How about the storage room?"

"No. Too much competition from the others."

"Right." He smiled. "The conference room?"

"The lieutenant holds meetings in there. Besides, walking around with evidence bags would draw curiosity. People would start asking questions."

"True." Ryan motioned toward the note. "Nadia said we had interviews set up for today. At what time?"

I studied the schedule on the note and drew in a quick breath. I immediately assumed that Nadia disliked me. "We have less than half an hour to get to the first one."

9

———————

We drove to the east end of Montreal to interview Marie's childhood friend, Judy White. The sixty-five-year-old was a retired schoolteacher. Based on information in our files, she had never married and had taught at primary and secondary schools for decades.

After Judy welcomed us into her condo, she chatted nonstop, stroking her small white dog who snuggled beside her on the sofa. The cute Westie rested his furry head on his paws, relaxing after his walk outdoors with her.

"I've lived in this condo for ten years," Judy said. "The area has changed a lot, but I love the convenience of having access to so many stores. Everything I need is steps away. It's practical when you're a senior and live alone. I feel safe living here too."

Safe, maybe, but her talkative behavior indicated nervousness to me. Was she uneasy about our visit or something else?

Ryan began the interview. "Judy, we'd like to talk to you about Marie Troy's disappearance in 1968."

Her hand flew to her chest. "Oh, my heavens! An officer contacted me about your visit, so I thought I was prepared. Yet every time I hear Marie's name, it brings back painful memories. It happened so long ago but..." She blinked. "I'm sorry. How can I help you, Sergeant?"

"Marie was supposed to meet you before school on the day she disappeared. Do you remember what happened?"

"I'll never forget it." She tucked strands of her chin-length white hair behind her ear. "I waited for Marie to meet me on the street corner like she did every weekday morning. We'd walk several blocks to school together. Since I was two years older than her, our mothers decided I'd be a suitable big sister." She smiled at the memory.

My attention briefly drifted to a bookshelf in the corner where high school yearbooks stood upright on the bottom shelf. Their consecutive order spanned over the last decade of her career. The memories of students, teachers, and school events during that period of Judy's career were obviously important to her.

Ryan interrupted my musing. "When Marie didn't show up that morning, what did you do?"

"Nothing, unfortunately," Judy said. "Marie hardly missed a day of school, so I thought she was sick and stayed home. Was I wrong about that." She sighed.

Ryan leaned forward, elbows resting on his knees. "When did you find out she was missing?"

"I stopped by her home after school to see if she was feeling better. You can imagine how surprised Mrs. Troy was when I told her Marie didn't go to school that day."

"What did Mrs. Troy do?"

"She called Marie's grandmother to find out if she was there. Of course, Marie wasn't there. Then Mrs. Troy called the school to confirm her attendance. There was some confusion. I can't remember what the problem was." Judy's brow crinkled. "Anyway, Mrs. Troy waited on the line for the longest time. Someone at the school finally told her they couldn't confirm if Marie had attended class that day. Mrs. Troy made more calls, maybe to family or a neighbor. Then she called the police. She was hysterical."

I marveled at Judy's relating of the details as seen through the eyes of her youth, though she'd left someone out of the picture. "We learned that Marie's younger brother, Tim, was home at the time," I said.

Judy winced. "Oh, my heavens, yes. He was inconsolable. His big sister was missing. We all cried together until the police arrived. I told the officer what I knew, then I went home and cried some more. I felt so guilty." Tears threatened to spill from her eyes even now.

I was a conduit for her pain. I felt the trauma and guilt she had endured and was still enduring. The crystal in my pocket lessened the anguish as I held onto it.

"Judy, would you know anyone who could have taken Marie?" Ryan asked. "Did you notice any suspicious persons hanging around the school or neighborhood around that time?"

"No. We were young kids. And innocent. We didn't think about things like that."

"Did you hang out with Marie after school?"

"No. I was two years older and had my own group of friends. I escorted Marie to school because our mothers knew each other. Marie's mother wanted to make sure she got to school safely." She looked down. "I failed on that promise."

"There was nothing you could have done," I empathized.

Judy's expression tightened. "Oh, yes there was. I could have gone to see Marie's mother right away instead of going to school that morning. She would have called the police sooner. They might have caught the person who kidnapped Marie." Tears welled in her eyes again and she blinked them back.

I tried to comfort her. "We don't know what happened to Marie, but it had nothing to do with you."

She wasn't buying it. "For days afterward, I blamed myself. I couldn't bear to face my school friends. The guilt was interfering with my grades too. Months later, my family moved to another part of the city. It meant a new school and a fresh start for me. But no matter how many years have passed, certain things are difficult to forget."

Judy's sorrow ran deep. From personal experience, I understood that the guilt we feel about someone's passing, whether justified or not, stays with us for a very long time. We try to make up for it in another way. Maybe Judy's choice of career as a schoolteacher was a promise to take care of other children to make up for the childhood friend she'd lost so long ago and still grieved.

Our next interview was with Sarina Bruno, Marie's former babysitter. Our quest took us to Kirkland, a suburb in the west end of Montreal, where landscaped parks, outdoor sports centers, and community events brought people together. Spacious lawns generated a sense of openness, while the dark clouds that had lingered since this morning threatened to burst at any moment.

In contrast, Sarina welcomed us into her two-story home with a cheery demeanor. She invited us to sit at the island in her spacious kitchen where the aroma of brewed coffee greeted us.

"Would you like a cup of coffee?" she asked.

We accepted.

Sarina made small talk as she placed our coffee mugs on the counter. "I raised two sons in this house. They spent half their days playing sports of one sort or another. Now they're raising families of their own." She pushed a strand of wispy blonde hair from her cheek.

Nervous chatting and movements were habits I'd noticed in witnesses. They weren't used to police interviewing them. I couldn't blame them. Police officers had an innate ability to make even innocent people feel guilty merely by their presence.

Sarina sipped her coffee, then set the mug down. She nervously fingered the handle. "I understand you wanted to talk to me about Marie Troy."

"That's right," Ryan said. "We've reopened her case. We're looking for information that might help us solve it."

She tensed up. "What kind of information?"

"Previous investigators reported that you used to babysit Marie. We're going back years now, but can you tell us when you last babysat her?"

Sarina briefly stared away, dredging up a memory. "It was the weekend before she went missing."

"Was it at the Troy home?" Ryan asked.

"Yes. Mrs. Troy had gone to a movie on Sunday afternoon with a female friend. She asked me to stay with Marie for a couple of hours."

"When did you hear about Marie's disappearance?"

"The day after she went missing."

Ryan checked the notes on his cell. "How did you find out?"

"I used to babysit other kids in the neighborhood," Sarina said. "One of their parents told me about it. I was terrified when I heard the news. Marie was such a sweetie. I lived across the lane from her and saw her on most mornings when she'd take the alley to school. It was a shorter path than going out her front door and around the block."

"Did you see Marie the morning she disappeared?"

"No, I was running late. I worked at a downtown clothing store and was rushing along the alley to get to the bus stop."

"Did you happen to see anything out of the ordinary that particular morning? A stranger or an unfamiliar vehicle in the alley?"

"Well..." Sarina chewed on her lip. "Not exactly a stranger, but I thought he was kind of creepy."

My heart pumped faster. "Who?"

"I already told investigators about him," she said. "He lived across the alley from me. His name is Gaston Belair."

It wasn't a coincidence that the same name kept popping up. I probed further. "Why did you think he was creepy?"

"Well, maybe not creepy," Sarina said, correcting herself. "Let's say he was quiet in a weird way. Even though he didn't say more than hello to me, he'd stare at me like he was undressing me before driving off in his pickup truck." She blushed. "Listen to me. I'm an old woman now, but trust me, I could turn heads back then." She giggled nervously.

Ryan smiled politely, then asked her, "Did you see Gaston the morning Marie disappeared?"

"Yes. Like I said, I was hurrying along the alley to the bus stop. He was backing out of his garage in his pickup truck. He said hello and waved as usual, then drove off."

"Did you notice anything in the back of his truck?"

Sarina shrugged. "The usual...tools, shovels."

"You don't sound sure."

"A tarp covered most of whatever was in the back of his truck. I'm guessing he had the same stuff I saw before when the truck was parked in his garage out back."

Ryan stayed on topic. "To clarify, you didn't speak much with Gaston. Correct?"

"No. To be honest, I was relieved he didn't try to have a long chat with me or ask me out on a date. Like I said, he was sort of weird. I moved into an apartment with a friend months later, so I never saw him again."

I took a chance to ask about another traveler in the alley. "There was a peddler who pulled a cart in the alley. Do you remember him?"

"Oh, my! That was ages ago." Sarina laughed. "Of course, I remember him."

"What can you tell us about him?"

"He was young, not more than twenty. He wore a flat cap and shabby clothes and had a scruffy dog. They do say dogs look like their owners." She smiled. "I saw him in the alley, combing through trash cans for stuff he could sell. I guess he had to support himself somehow."

"Did you ever speak to him?"

"No, but I saw him stop to speak with Gaston in his garage a couple of times." She paused, bringing another memory to light. "Some mothers had warned their children not to have anything to do with the peddler, but they gathered around him anyway. They were attracted to his dog, I suppose. Several of the older kids liked to tease him, though. They'd shout at him, 'Ragman, full of fleas,' then run away. The kids provoked him. I felt sorry for the man."

Mrs. Troy had told us how the peddler had reacted to the teasing, but I wanted Sarina's version. "What did he do? Did he ever get angry?"

Sarina's eyes widened. "You bet. He jumped down from his cart and chased a boy once." At my astonished look, she added, "Oh, don't worry, he didn't catch him. When the boy ran into a backyard on my side of the alley, the peddler returned to his cart."

Ryan asked, "Did any of your neighbors see other instances of the peddler behaving out of the ordinary?"

"Not that I heard. Sometimes he'd go by late at night or before dawn. His cart didn't make as much noise as a vehicle, but I'm a light sleeper and I'd hear it in the alley. He stopped coming by soon after Marie..." She stopped. "I guess he got a real job or something."

～

As we drove away, I said to Ryan, "Can you imagine a grubby peddler running after little kids? It must have been terrifying for them."

He agreed. "That's the second witness report we got on him. He sounds like an aggressive type. I hope Nadia or Corey can track him down."

"For all we know, he could be a million miles away." Our discussion with Sarina sparked a memory. "Wait. Didn't Sarina say she saw Gaston talking to him? If we can find Gaston—"

"Then we might be able to locate the mystery peddler," Ryan said, completing my thought.

I had an idea. "Remember how Mrs. Troy said Gaston's old house was up for sale? We should take a drive there. I might be able to get a perception about what kind of man he was."

"But he doesn't live there anymore."

"It doesn't matter. We don't have to go inside."

"Okay. I'll see what I can do." The spark of hope in Ryan's voice told me he was counting on this potential lead as much as I was.

10

———

We launched Marie Troy's page on the police website the next morning. Corey cheered, and Nadia clapped her hands in a rare show of emotion when the site went live. Anticipation inspired the send-off, but persistence would have to drive it forward.

Another upside was that a crew was working this weekend on a video reenactment of Marie's kidnapping. Since videos brought in more calls to the Info-Crime line, there was a chance that someone would come forward with an unexpected clue.

Keen on obtaining news about any progress our unit made on current cold cases, Lieutenant Payton often circled our group like a buzzard. His presence was a reminder that we had to make the best of our limited time and resources to solve cases. We now held our collective breaths as he observed the photos and age-progression sketches of Marie Troy displayed on her site.

"Kudos." The lieutenant gave a thumbs-up to the team. Then he confidently retreated to his office to report back to his superiors.

Despite our initial optimism, the lieutenant's praise was

fleeting. After I reviewed the scant facts that we'd managed to scrape together for Marie's page, my excitement wavered. I'd supported Ryan's suggestion that we hold back from releasing certain pieces of evidence, such as the ring on a gold chain that Marie had worn every day. Yet now, I was reconsidering it.

What if the jewelry was with her remains, hidden in an isolated area too difficult to locate? What good would it do to keep that piece of information from the public?

Ryan explained that investigators usually withheld information from the public as a safeguard. If the jewelry was with Marie's remains, only the real killer would know that detail. Withholding information also prevented imposters from claiming they committed the deed, if only to gain attention.

Satisfied with his reasoning, I was ready to move on. Despite the lack of solid evidence, our investigation wasn't over. We needed to interview more witnesses, some of whom we hadn't been able to contact so far, namely Gaston Belair and the unknown peddler in the alley. Like other witnesses we'd interviewed, these two men had been known to Marie and had lived in or visited her neighborhood. I was eager to meet with them to get insights into their behavior.

~

That afternoon, we were on the road again. Ryan had made arrangements with a real estate agent to visit Gaston Belair's old house. It was still on the market, but I wasn't interested in the house. I was curious about Gaston. Witnesses we'd interviewed had described him as quiet, a hard worker, or an ogler. I was relying on his vacated home to talk to me. If it could trigger my perceptions, I could find out what kind of man he truly was.

Ryan drove past several empty lots. He parked in front of a three-story row house where the real estate agent stood waiting for us, his navy raincoat flapping in the wind. A faded For Sale sign on the lawn tilted to the right, about to topple. The agent hadn't straightened it, which said a lot about his lack of interest in showing the house to prospective buyers.

After I stepped out of the car and looked up at the house, an eerie sensation spread over me. My hands felt numb and tingly, but the feeling passed as quickly as it had begun. Spontaneous feelings were difficult to explain, and I didn't want to jump to conclusions.

I took in the view. The front lawn hadn't been cut in weeks and was strewn with litter. A second-floor window was cracked, and another was boarded up. So much for curb appeal. Maybe the inside was more promising.

Without disclosing our connection to the police, we shook hands with Barry Eckerd, the real estate agent. In his mid-thirties with well-coiffed hair that had been set with finishing spray, Barry kept the conversation short. He rapidly led us up a pebbly path to the house, giving me the impression that he had no time to waste.

At the front door, Barry pulled out a set of keys from his pocket. "This house has been on the market much longer than most. I told the owner that similar buildings were selling for much less. He refused to budge on the price. Stubborn old geezer." He smirked and unlocked the door, then gave it a hard push to open it. It groaned, as if it were in pain.

A musty smell greeted us in the entrance. I immediately felt queasy, but it wasn't from the smell. Feeling a wave of apprehension, I fought the urge to turn around and hurry back outside. Instead, I discreetly slipped my hand around the crystal in my jacket and concentrated on the conversation.

"Sorry about the odor." Uneasiness crossed Barry's face. "I don't visit here often, so it's been closed up for a while."

I sensed he wasn't being truthful about the smell.

We entered the living room on the left. Scratches on a dull wood floor indicated where pieces of furniture had once stood. Not to be outdone, a crack in the ceiling spread diagonally from one corner to the other, prompting fears that the building might collapse at any moment.

"I'll be blunt," Barry said. "This house needs a lot of work."

An unexpected insight of a little girl playing with a dog flashed before me. She had her back to me and was giggling. She was blonde, so it could have been Marie or any other little girl. Regardless, it was comforting. I'd tell Ryan about it later.

We followed Barry along a narrow hallway lined with a tattered brown carpet. A peek inside two empty bedrooms revealed the same dated yellow linoleum on both floors. A different flowery wallpaper barely clinging to the walls in each room begged for mercy.

"I see what you mean about a lot of work," Ryan said.

"You've probably noticed the empty lots on this street," Barry said. "The homes in this area were built in the 1950s. The weak structure and wear and tear over the years have attracted developers. They hope to cash in on the falling property values to tear them down and build new homes."

"Sounds like a reasonable option."

"Why are you interested in this particular house, if you don't mind my asking?"

Ryan winged it. "We're searching the market for an inexpensive investment property."

Barry raised an eyebrow. "Oh? For renovation purposes?"

"It depends on the price."

"I have to tell you that we already have a potential buyer who wants to buy this property and the adjacent empty lots as well. If the deal goes through, he'll obtain a permit to demolish this house soon. He wants to build a larger structure on the combined lots. Of course, should you want to place a bid—"

"Thanks. I'll take it into consideration."

"Fine." Barry continued down the hallway.

Ryan gave me a subtle smile before we moved along. He was clearly enjoying the ploy.

As soon as we entered the kitchen at the back of the house,

a damp, putrid scent inflamed my nose. I didn't dare open any of the cabinets in case a rodent had died there. "Whew!" I waved a hand in the air.

"The windows haven't been opened lately," Barry said in his defense again. He proceeded to point out the warped linoleum, the dated cabinets, and discolored walls that hinted at mold. "Let me give you some honest advice. Unless you plan on taking down this place, you'll need an army of restoration experts to bring it up to a viable level for resale."

To say the least. How Gaston Belair, a repairman by trade, could have neglected this house to such an extent amazed me.

A glimpse out the window into the backyard revealed patches of weeds protruding through pebbles. Gone was any hint that a grassy lawn might have once covered the ground. A separate garage with cement walls bordered the far end of the yard and blocked most of the view to the alley beyond. Even here, the view told a dismal story.

The ambiance in the air changed without warning. Depression, terror, grief. A mix of emotions that I couldn't explain washed over me. Then a flash of red exploded in my line of sight, sending shivers down my spine. I had to escape from this horrendous place!

Barry pushed open the back door. "If you'd like to see the backyard and the garage—"

Trembling, I whispered to Ryan, "I need to get out of here!"

I could barely contain my panic. I turned and flew down the hallway and out the front door. Thrusting my hand in my pocket to clasp the amethyst crystal, I took deep gulps of air. Only then did I realize it had started to rain. I stepped back under the shelter of the overhang.

The front door creaked open behind me and the men stepped out.

"Here's my card." Barry handed it to Ryan. "Let me know what you decide." To me he said, "Hope you feel better soon." He pulled up the collar of his raincoat and rushed to his car.

"Did you tell him I was sick?" I asked Ryan.

"No." He gave me a sheepish grin. "I told him you had allergies to something in there."

I smiled. "Whatever works, I suppose. Can we go now?"

We raced through the downpour to the sanctuary of the car.

As we buckled up, Ryan turned to me, concern in his eyes. "Want to share what happened back there, Amber?"

I told him about my impression of a happy little girl playing with a dog.

"That's incredible. Mrs. Troy told us Marie visited here. Was it her?"

"She was blonde like Marie, but I couldn't see her face. She was standing with her back to me."

"Anything else?"

"I saw a flash of red when I looked out at the backyard. It lasted less than a second, but it filled me with terror."

"What does it mean?"

"I'm not sure. It might be a warning or a sign."

Ryan started the engine. "A sign of what?"

"I don't know," I said. "These things are hard to analyze." The disappointment on his face prompted me to come up with a possible explanation. "Maybe a rodent died in there. It did smell pretty awful."

He wrinkled his nose. "Yeah."

Gaston's house triggered a memory. "Mrs. Troy told us that Gaston had done repair jobs for her and other neighbors. She seemed to trust him. And yet, Sarina, Marie's babysitter, found him creepy."

He grinned. "Some guys can appear to be creepy. They're not all killers, though."

"I get that people are innocent until proven guilty. Even so, we should keep Gaston in mind as a potential suspect. What if he lured Marie to his house that morning?"

Ryan steered the car through the traffic. "Let's consider that theory. Assume that Gaston talked to Marie after she visited her grandmother. Let's say he invited her inside to play with his dog before she went to school. He could have convinced her it would only be for a few minutes. Let's suppose he knocked her out somehow, or worse. It would have been easy to carry an unconscious little girl from his house, put her in his pickup truck in the garage, and drive away."

"I doubt he'd carry Marie outside in broad daylight," I said. "Someone in an upper-floor residence could have seen him. Anyway, Sarina saw Gaston drive off early that morning. Would he have had the time to do all that?"

He nodded. "Interesting points. Let's consider another theory. If Gaston killed Marie in his house that morning, he probably waited until he could dispose of her body unseen, like at nighttime."

It was my turn to put a damper on the conversation. "Day or night, what does it matter anyway?"

"What do you mean?"

I threw my arms up in frustration. "How can we prove anyone is guilty of murder without a body?"

11

Unexpected news awaited us when we returned to the police station. It was the break we'd been waiting for.

Corey had tracked down Gaston Belair through an obscure address on one of his speeding tickets on record. The address belonged to a business that he operated from a low-rise condo in the city of Laval, the largest suburb of Montreal. The nature of the business wasn't listed.

With no time to stop for lunch, Ryan and I drove straight there without notifying Gaston. The element of surprise had worked in our favor before. We were confident it would work again.

As predicted, Gaston Belair's jaw dropped when he opened the door and Ryan pulled out his badge. He hastily recovered and invited us inside.

In his mid-seventies, with hands that could easily grasp a football in each, Gaston had a muscular build that people half his age would envy. "I traded my construction tools for these babies." A broad wave of his hand encompassed a treadmill, a stationary bicycle, and various weights that took up most of the space in his living room.

Ryan surveyed the equipment. "Impressive. It keeps you in shape."

"You bet. I'm in great shape. I'd be working in construction today if I hadn't fallen off a faulty ladder and broken my leg twenty years ago. It didn't heal properly, so I couldn't go back to work at Torg Construction."

Ryan pretended he didn't know that Gaston operated a business from his condo. "If you're not working, how do you manage to pay for the upkeep here?"

"My old age pension helps. I also use my contacts in the industry to find jobs for other construction workers. In turn, they pay me a finder's fee or compensate me in other ways."

"Other ways?" I repeated. "How?"

"They buy me groceries or do small favors," Gaston said. "Tit for tat, as they say." He chuckled.

The widescreen TV on the wall wasn't bought with grocery money. Either he wasn't truthful, or his finder's fees were higher than I imagined.

Gaston put his hands on his hips. "Sergeant, you came here unannounced. It can't be about my speeding tickets because I paid them."

Ryan cut to the topic. "We're investigating a cold case from 1968. A little girl named Marie Troy went missing on her way to school one morning." He dug out his phone and showed Gaston a school photo of her.

I focused on Gaston, hoping to pick up the slightest sign of nervousness. I saw none.

Instead, his dark eyes glinted with awareness. "Ah yes, I remember her disappearance very well. Her mother was my neighbor. Bernadette. Poor woman."

Ryan went on. "We have it on record that former investigators questioned you about Marie."

"Me and everyone else on the street. I was working at a construction site that day. The police asked my boss at Torg to confirm it and he did."

Ryan checked his notes. "We suspect that Marie went missing between eight and eight thirty that morning. There's a time gap in your schedule. You reported to work at Torg Construction at noon. Where were you before that?"

"I was probably working on a job for someone else," Gaston said.

"Who?"

The furrows across Gaston's forehead deepened. "Are you serious? You think I remember those kinds of details after all these years?" He softened his tone. "Look, Sergeant, I'm an old man. My memory has faded over time. I did a lot of odd jobs and repairs back then, like mounting drywall or putting up wood beams."

"Investigators interviewed other people in your old neighborhood." Ryan was careful not to disclose that we'd recently met with Sarina. "There's an eyewitness account that you spoke with a peddler who went through trash cans in the alley."

"Oh, you mean Eddie Doyle," Gaston said.

Eddie Doyle! We finally had a name for the mystery man. I hid my excitement.

Ryan remained cool and played along. "That's right. Eddie Doyle."

"Eddie was going through a rough patch," Gaston said. "He asked me if I had work for him."

"Did you?"

"I brought him to the construction site to meet my boss. He hired Eddie to work on projects."

"Can you tell us more about Eddie? Was he a good worker?"

"How the hell would I know?" Gaston scoffed. "I just introduced him to the boss, that's all. I wasn't his babysitter." His tone mellowed. "I didn't know him personally. He wanted to make a few bucks like the rest of us, so I helped him. It gave me a warm feeling inside. That's why I continue helping others get jobs even today."

"Do you know how we can reach Eddie?" Ryan asked.

"No. Like I said, I helped him get work in the past. That's all it was, but in the end…" He gave his head a shake. "What I'm trying to say is, you do a guy like him a favor and hope he'll turn his life around. In Eddie's case, it didn't work out."

"What do you mean?"

"After working for Torg, he went back to his old ways. You know…drinking and drugs and stuff. He was a sneaky guy, basically living on the street…stealing…hanging out with the wrong crowd… That's the last I heard."

Ryan tucked his phone in his pocket. "We understand your old property is for sale."

"Man, you guys are thorough." Gaston grinned. "Yeah, the agent is having a tough time selling it. But the price is fair. I didn't want to waste my time trying to fix the building because it's rat infested. I killed a bunch of those buggers myself, but they kept coming back, even after the exterminators came. I couldn't live there anymore. I know the developers want to buy it. They would demolish it anyway." As he moved slightly to one side, his foot hit a pair of thirty-pound weights. He casually picked them up and placed them several feet out of the way.

I was still trying to process the fact that Gaston had killed rats. It could explain the smell and the red flash I experienced when Ryan and I toured his old home. While I sensed he was telling the truth, my instincts told me it wasn't the whole story.

"Did you ever invite Marie Troy into your home?" Ryan had circled back to our original topic, catching Gaston off guard.

He jerked. "What? Why would I do that?"

"So she could play with your dog."

Gaston's eyes narrowed. "What are you getting at?"

Silence increased the tension in the air as the two men attempted to outstare each other. Would Gaston cut short our visit?

I jumped in. "Marie lived near your old home, Gaston. Did you see her the day she disappeared or invite her into your home?"

He pointed at me. "No, and I didn't touch that girl, okay? I was busy working at the construction company and on projects for other clients. End of story."

Since I had his attention, I pushed forward. "Did you ever give Marie a ride to school?"

Gaston clenched his jaw. "I have nothing more to say to either of you. I'll see you out." He plodded toward the door.

~

As we headed back to the car, Ryan said, "That was pretty daring of you."

I looked at him. "Oh. Are you going to give me another lecture now?"

"Not at all. I wish I would have asked Gaston those questions." He threw me a side glance. "What are you so uptight about, Amber?"

"Remember the impression I got when I held Louise Lavoie's Snoopy toy? About choking in a dark place?"

"Yes. What about it?"

"The real estate agent had mentioned that developers might demolish Gaston's old house. Now Gaston mentioned it too. Maybe what I perceived at his old house was the dust and debris from the demolition...suffocating me."

Ryan stopped walking and stared at me. "Hang on a sec, Amber. Are you making a connection between Gaston and Louise's abduction now? You think he kidnapped her and hid her body in his old house?"

The way he said it sounded ridiculous even to me. "Well..."

"You have to admit it's a bit of a stretch."

"Okay, but Gaston wasn't telling us everything."

"It doesn't matter. He's on our radar. So is our next witness." Ryan pulled out his phone and called the station. "Corey, get me all the info you can on Edward Doyle or Eddie Doyle."

12

Eddie Doyle's two-story home in Montreal North was a ten-minute drive from the station. While Corey confirmed that Eddie owned another property outside Montreal, he also discovered a criminal record on file for the former junk collector. Like our impromptu trip to interview Gaston, Ryan thought it best if we didn't alert Eddie about our arrival beforehand.

At first, Eddie hesitated to invite us inside. I assumed his criminal record might have made him guarded about speaking with the police. When Ryan stated the purpose of our visit and finally coaxed him to let us in, I understood why Eddie had been reluctant.

The living room was littered with clothes, books, cookware, cardboard boxes, and plastic containers. A familiar refrain kept running through my head: Old habits die hard. The heaps of clutter implied that Eddie was a hoarder, though his personal health appeared to fare much better. Slim and muscular, the senior had short white hair and was clean-shaven.

Ryan showed Eddie a photo of Marie Troy on his cell. "This young girl went missing in 1968."

Eddie gave him a guarded look. "I don't know nothin' about

that missing girl. I don't even know her name or where she lived."

"You were seen going through the garbage in the alley behind her house for years. The kids teased you and called you names. You even chased after them."

Eddie stiffened. "Those kids rubbed me the wrong way."

Ryan pressed on. "Did you see Marie Troy the morning she disappeared?"

"I saw kids every day, but I didn't know their names."

"I asked you a specific question."

Eddie's face flushed with anger. "I already told you, I didn't see the girl you're talkin' about."

"Did you notice any suspicious activity on your, um, route?"

"Nah. There wasn't much traffic in those lanes."

Ryan studied the notes on his cell. "I checked your police file, Eddie. Burglary...petty theft."

"Hey, I had no family to help me. A guy's gotta eat. It got tough, goin' through town, lookin' for scraps to sell. Even sellin' off the best items I found in the garbage couldn't feed me on some days."

Ryan used a bogus tactic to draw more information. "The day Marie disappeared, a witness saw you speaking with Gaston Belair in the alley. That ring any bells?"

Eddie's eyes reflected surprise. "So what? Ain't nothin' wrong with talkin' to people."

"We interviewed Gaston today. He mentioned how he gave you a helping hand."

"Oh, yeah. I almost forgot about that. He got me workin' for Torg Construction. It didn't last too long, though."

"Why not?"

Eddie sighed. "I got tired of doin' favors for Gaston on account that he got me contract work. He never let me forget his so-called generosity to me. I'm sure glad I kept my day job." He chuckled and waved toward the disorderly room.

I recalled how a neighbor had found Marie's schoolbag in

the garbage and handed it to the police. I kept my tone light as I asked Eddie, "Did you find anything special in the alley the day Marie vanished?"

He paled, as if I'd discovered something he was trying to cover up. "Like what?"

I used Ryan's sly tactic to imply that my next statement was true. "A witness saw you going through the garbage in the alley by Marie's home the day she went missing."

"Oh...well..." Eddie hesitated. "I suppose I was lookin' for the usual stuff. Chipped dishware, old lamps..." He perked up. "You know, those things are antiques today and worth a lot of money, even if they have a tiny crack in them."

Ryan asked, "Is that how you could afford to buy this house?"

"Nah. Fate awarded me for savin' my pennies."

"How?"

"I won the lottery decades ago." Eddie smiled, adding more wrinkles to his face.

"The lottery?" Ryan said in disbelief.

"Yeah. I bought a lakeside home, but there was a problem. No one told me heavy rains flooded the area every couple of years. I repaired the moldy walls myself and sold it. Then I bought this house and a business outside Montreal. I called it Eddie's Orchard."

I'd heard of the popular orchard. Families flocked there every fall.

Eddie went on. "You know, I didn't buy the orchard only to make money. I bought it so people can come and pick their own basket of apples for a dollar. It was my way of givin' back to the community. I did so well, I'm buildin' an extension at the orchard for storage."

A sudden flash of red crossed my vision. *No, not again!* What did it mean?

Ryan put away his cell. "I have a suggestion for you, Eddie. Visit Marie Troy's page on our police website. It might jog your memory. Here's my business card." He handed it to him. "My advice to you in the meantime? Don't leave town. We might have more questions for you."

Eddie led us to the front door and said, "Good luck with your case, Sergeant. I hope you find out what happened to that little girl for the family's sake."

On our drive back to the station, Ryan clenched the steering wheel. "Did you see the show Eddie put on for us? All compassionate about giving back to the community. Give me a break."

"I sensed he was hiding something," I said, "but I don't know what."

"Did you get any other insights back there?"

"Yes. A flash of red again. I can't explain why I saw it when we were with Gaston Belair and now with Eddie Doyle. I've come to accept it as a sign that something about them is connected to the cases we're investigating."

Ryan said nothing. Like me, he was weighing the possibility that one of these men might turn out to be a prime suspect in a child's abduction.

Back at my desk, I opened up Marie's website page to see if there were any comments from the public. There were none. Just questions from curiosity seekers and false leads with incorrect timelines.

I was about to call it a day—or evening, since it was seven o'clock—and drive home, when Matt made a noisy entrance. He bustled toward Ryan and me. "Glad you're both here. I've been knocking on doors all day, interviewing anyone who lived in the same area as Louise." He dropped a slim portfolio on his desk, then slumped in his chair and loosened his tie.

Ryan leaned forward. "What have you got?"

"Sore feet." Matt sulked. He opened his portfolio and leafed through the pages inside. "I must have a hundred names here.

Many people have moved away. Others hadn't heard of a missing girl named Louise Lavoie. To recap, I covered a lot of ground but got zilch to show for it. I'll give Corey a copy of all the names I collected so he can run them through the criminal database. I have a hunch nothing will come of it."

Ryan sat back. "Then we'll go to plan B."

"You had a plan B and didn't tell me? What's plan B?"

"First thing Monday, get together with Nadia and Corey to develop a contact page for Louise on the police website. Include photos, age progression sketches...whatever it takes. They'll know what to do."

Matt gawked at him. "You mean I did all that legwork for nothing?"

Ryan ignored his question. "While Nadia and Corey set up Louise's page, Amber and I will sit with you to discuss the similarities between our two cases. We'll develop a strategy from there."

"Fine." Matt stood up, adjusted his pants over a protruding stomach. "Anyone want to grab a beer? Dinner?"

"Count me out," Ryan said. "I need to finish a pile of reports." He slid his chair closer to his desk.

"I'm going home." I picked up my things. "See you guys tomorrow." As I walked away, I could hear Matt trying to convince Ryan to opt for a pizza delivery.

I contemplated the progress of our team on the drive home. Here we were, three investigators with two ongoing investigations. Despite the subtle fairy-tale connotation and other similarities in both cases, none of us had come up with evidence to link the victims to a feasible suspect.

Oh, sure, Ryan and I had interviewed Gaston and Eddie and considered them to be persons of interest in Marie Troy's case. Our suspicions meant nothing, though, since either of these men could argue they were simply in the wrong place at the wrong time. We weren't any closer to proving their involvement in the crime.

We needed answers and fast. It would be wishful thinking to expect that a lead would come in through the Info-Crime line. Such calls were rare, especially for cold cases. No, we needed someone or something to guide us in the right direction. In short, we needed a miracle. Come Monday, the lieutenant would be circling us like a vulture in search of a positive progress report to feed his expectations and those of his superiors.

On second thought, there *was* someone I could turn to for help.

Laura King, accomplished psychologist, historian, and my secret confidante, was invaluable when it came to shedding light on the hidden aspects of criminal cases. As an expert in fairy-tale studies and interpretation, she'd assisted me with the Vicky Johnson case. I was confident she would help me again.

But it was the weekend. I'd have to wait until Monday to speak with her.

13

———

Devoting Saturday mornings to volunteer work at local hospitals and retirement homes was the perfect ending to my workweek. Reading to sick kids and ailing seniors brought me personal satisfaction. The visits also restored positive energy to my life that the negative energy of the cold cases drained from me.

I enjoyed visiting the children at General Hospital. It satisfied my need to bring happiness into their lives. It also reminded me how much I wanted to protect every child from harm, which was something I couldn't do until all predators were behind bars.

I appreciated that today's group of four-year-old kids looked forward to my visit. "Goldilocks and the Three Bears" generated laughter from Jimmy, despite his broken arm. I treasured Zoey's wide-eyed interest and Nina's animated expressions as they absorbed the dramatic scenes in "Little Red Riding Hood," the second story they chose. Despite their reactions, I could barely get through reading the story without thinking about Marie Troy. For a second, I pictured a slightly younger Marie sitting among the others and listening as enthusiastically as they were.

I'd finished reading "Hansel and Gretel," the third story the young group had selected, when a hospital attendant wheeled in a snack tray. My visit was over. I grabbed my handbag, hugged the kids goodbye, and set out for my next visit at Larkspur Retirement Community.

A short drive later, I knocked at the door to Mrs. Brody's room. I had a special connection to the petite woman: She was Ryan's mother.

Mrs. Brody preferred to use her maiden name after her husband had passed away, which was a comfort to Ryan. "I worry less that an angry convict I put away might seek revenge by seeking out my mother," he'd once told me.

Mrs. Brody opened the door and greeted me with a smile. "Oh, hello, Natasha. So lovely to see you again."

Although she recognized me, her dementia was the reason she dubbed me with a different name whenever I visited her. I smiled back and said nothing about it.

As I entered, a floral scent filled the air. I traced the aroma to a bouquet of flowers on the coffee table. "Those flowers are beautiful, Mrs. Brody."

"My son gave them to me," she said, leading me toward the armchairs we usually occupied during my readings. "He knows how much I love roses and lilies. Don't you, dear?" She looked to the left.

Out of my line of sight, Ryan had been standing near a window on the other side of the room. "Hi...uh...Natasha."

"Oh, excuse my manners, dear," Mrs. Brody said to me. "This is my son." Her gaze swung from me to Ryan and back again.

Ryan came up to me and shook my hand. "Nice to meet you." He smiled and squeezed my hand.

"Same here." I squeezed back.

"You know, you two would make such a lovely couple." Mrs. Brody chuckled, then said to Ryan, "Why don't you ask her out on a date, dear?"

"I might do that one day." He zipped up his jacket and dug out his key fob.

Mrs. Brody stared at him. "Where are you going? You just got here."

"No, Mom. I've been here an hour."

"Oh." Mrs. Brody cast a puzzled look at the floor.

Ryan kissed her on the cheek. "I'll come visit you again soon." He gave me a subtle wink before he walked out.

～

"You see?" Ryan said, pouring more wine into our glasses during dinner. "Thanks to my mother's matchmaking efforts, we would have ended up together anyway."

I laughed. "She's a real darling. And so are you. Thanks for cooking dinner tonight. This lasagna is delicious."

"My pleasure. It's the least I could do after all the meals you prepared for me in this house."

"You earned them. You helped me bring my parents' home back to life again. Look at this place." I gestured widely. "All the repair work and painting... I couldn't have done it without you."

"On the subject of this house..." He took a sip of wine, then put down his glass. "We haven't spoken about this lately. Are you still having bad dreams about...you know?"

Ryan knew all about the recurring nightmares I'd experienced since my youth. "I have them once in a while. It depends on the type of case I'm working on. The victim and evidence can trigger them."

"Yeah, criminal investigations can be gruesome. Vicky's Johnson's kidnapping case was a tough start for us."

I drank some wine. "I'll say."

"How you almost lost your life when you lured Vicky's perp into a police trap was the worst part." He shook his head. "The lieutenant shouldn't have agreed to put you in that position."

"It was my idea. It was the only way we could have caught LT."

We'd taken the habit of referring to the formidable opponent by his initials after his capture because we didn't deem him human enough to merit a name. It had been our deliberate choice to render inhuman one of the worst child kidnappers and murderers of all time.

Ryan continued to reminisce. "Vicky's case was one of the biggest the Montreal Police had ever cracked. And we did it. You and me. Here's to us."

"To us." I clinked his glass with mine.

"The unit is slowly expanding. Now Matt is on board." He took a bite of lasagna.

"He seems to be trying hard to make a positive impression."

"He needs reining in. He has a tendency to be impetuous."

"You mean, like wanting to interview the suspects in Marie's case?" I swallowed a forkful of the layered pasta.

"It's more personal than that," Ryan said. "When we worked together in homicide, he rushed through witness reports and missed important details in his hurry to solve the case. He occasionally investigated on his own and didn't share his findings with me, like he was trying to one-up me. Since he divorced, and his wife has full custody of the kids, it's as if he wants to make up for his personal loss by proving himself on the job."

I didn't mention how Matt had flirted with me in the kitchen. It wasn't worth causing a larger rift between them. I was sure I'd quashed any future advances from Matt anyway. "He wants to show his work has merit, that he's valuable to the unit."

"Don't get me wrong. Matt is one heck of a decent cop, but he's new to the job. He hasn't investigated cold cases before."

"A divorce can be tough. His work could be all he has to occupy him now. He needs input from someone more experienced. Like you."

"Could be. Working in a different department does present somewhat of a learning curve."

Another coworker came to mind. "By the way, I'm afraid that Nadia might be catching onto us."

Worry lines spread across Ryan's forehead. "Us? How?"

"The other day, when we were alone in the office...after you kissed me. She walked in with Corey. She might have seen us."

"It's my fault. I'll have to be more careful in the future." He took a gulp of his wine.

"Nadia is very observant. And curious. She noticed my reactions when I held the evidence. She's starting to question that too. We should tell her and Corey what it is that I actually do."

"Not yet," he said. "The less people know about you, the safer you'll be."

I ate more lasagna while I contemplated his comment. "Are you saying you don't trust Nadia and Corey? They're already sworn to secrecy about the kind of work they do."

"I trust them. It's not that. It's just"—Ryan reached over and held my hand—"I worry about you and the people out there who see you as an easy target."

A loving, protective feeling enveloped me. "It goes both ways, Ryan. I worry about you too. You're not exactly invisible to your enemies."

"Right on." He laughed, then let go of my hand. "We'll take it one day at a time. Let's see what develops next week." He paused. "What also concerns me is the lieutenant. He expects results on our cases soon, or our jobs will be on the line."

"We've completed all our interviews. From what Matt told us, so has he. What more can we do? Wait for a tip to come in through the Info-Crime line?"

"Like I told Matt, we'll get together with him on Monday to compare notes on both our cases. From what I've seen, there are similarities in the perp's profile in each." He glanced at my empty plate. "Ready for dessert?"

Ryan made a sincere effort to lighten the conversation the rest of the evening but, like me, I suspected that the uncertainty of the unit's future and our jobs lurked at the back of his mind.

14

———————

Saturday night rolled into Sunday. I was eager to spend a fun afternoon with Nicole. She usually had interesting tales to tell me about her young students at Blessed Mary Elementary School, the primary school where she taught. Her apartment building was several blocks from my house, and it was my turn to visit her. It was a sunny day, so I walked over.

Modular sofas, abstract paintings in vivid yellows and blues, an arched floor lamp, a soft rug underfoot... The décor in Nicole's apartment was a sharp contrast to the traditional style in my home. My excuse was that most of my furniture came with the house that I inherited from my parents. Aside from purchasing a modern sofa and throw pillows when I started to work as a police consultant, I planned to replace the old dining room set next.

Nicole and I settled on a leather sectional in her living room with a bowl of potato chips between us. Since she liked to shop for home décor, I examined the room for anything new. A six-foot rubber plant beside the flat screen TV didn't disappoint.

"Oh, you got a new plant," I said.

"It's not a *real* one," Nicole said, rolling the "r" in her endearing French accent. "I don't have to water it. Someone gave it to me." She crunched into a potato chip.

She was holding something back. "Someone? Which someone?" I teased.

She laughed. "Oh, Amber, it's not what you think. He's a teacher at the school. A very nice *old* teacher. I helped him move into a new apartment last weekend, so he gave me this plant to thank me." Her eyes twinkled. "Enough about me. How are you and Ryan doing these days?"

"We're good."

Amusement edged her voice. "You can't fool me, Amber. You seem so happy. Are you in love?"

"It's not like that. We're close but it's not serious."

"Not serious? What kind of relationship is that?"

Nicole was one of the few people I hung out with, and I treasured her friendship. I also trusted her. I decided to confide in her about my prohibited relationship at work.

"So you and Ryan…it's forbidden," she said, dismayed. "Oh, Amber, I'm so sorry. It must be so hard for you."

"Not really. We manage to see each other on the outside. Secretly, of course." I sought escape and brought up another topic. "By the way, how are your students? Any funny experiences you want to share?"

"Something funny happens every day with those kids. And the stories they tell me." She laughed. "Oh, yes! I have exciting news. The school planned an event for next week. Several classes will be visiting an apple farm located about thirty miles north of here. It's called Eddie's Orchard. Have you ever heard of it?"

Eddie's Orchard. I almost choked on my soda pop. "Yes. It's quite popular with families."

"Great!" Nicole's face lit up with enthusiasm. "We were so lucky to book a visit. The orchard is really busy. The kids are so excited about the field trip. They'll get free apple tarts to take home. School buses will take us there and..."

I half listened as she went on about how the kids would have so much fun at the orchard. Fun or not, my guard was up. Was I making too much of the coincidence?

The conversation soon moved to which movie we should watch. Even though Nicole and I were about the same age, the kind of movies we watched together were on the tame side. It was my fault. I'd held back from revealing my psychic gift and resulting emotional sensitivities to her. As a result, she believed that my avoidance of violent or horror movies was because I couldn't tolerate gory or shocking scenes. She also took my avoidance of crowds and busy places as an anxiety disorder, which meant we either got together at her place or mine, not a busy club or restaurant. I left it at that.

After we watched a romantic comedy, Nicole insisted that I stay longer, so I did. We chose a second movie: an old Agatha Christie mystery.

Soon it was time for me to leave. We promised to get together again in the coming weeks.

"And let me know if it gets more serious between you and Ryan," she said, smiling. "I want all the delicious details."

Ryan meant a lot to me, but I wasn't ready to admit it to anyone. "Have fun at the orchard with the kids," I said, my parting words suddenly sounding hollow to me. What on earth was bothering me?

A chilly autumn wind had swept the day away. I raised the collar of my jacket and wished I'd have driven to Nicole's instead of taking the sun's rays for granted earlier.

A glance around told me there was no one else on the street this blustery evening. And yet, I felt someone's eyes on my back.

I spun around. No one.

"Stop," I told myself. "You're not that scared little girl hiding in a closet anymore."

In spite of efforts to convince myself that I was safe, the feeling that someone was watching me lingered. Maybe Ryan was right about me being a target. My heart pounded as I ran the rest of the way home.

15

———————

A heavy rainfall system swept through the city Monday morning, like an eagle swooping in on its target. That I'd had a restless sleep the night before, waking when images of shadowy creatures broke into my dreams, did nothing to lighten my mood. The result was a gloomy attitude and a foggy brain.

I couldn't blame the suspenseful movie I'd watched at Nicole's last night for my tossing and turning. No, this was my own doing, my own fears returning from the past, which I'd failed to control.

Previous visits with psychologist and historian Laura King had revealed why my self-conscious mind kept stirring up these alarming nightmares. It was all about the guilt I felt after my parents had been killed. They'd prevented an intruder from kidnapping me when I was five years old and died while protecting me. Those were the hard facts that kept running through my mind, embedded in there for eternity.

As was my habit, I dropped by Laura's office at eight o'clock in the morning, before her first scheduled appointment with a client and before my day shift at the station. She'd been one of my mother's closest friends, and despite our age differences, she offered me that same friendship and an open-door policy whenever I sought her guidance. As one of the trusted people of my inner circle, she protected my secret, and I hers.

Laura peered at me over the rim of her eyeglasses. "I haven't seen you in months."

Although it wasn't a question, I felt as if I owed her an explanation. "I've been busy...working with police investigators on cases...doing home renovations..."

Too polite to rebuff my miserable excuses, Laura asked her usual question, "Are you still having disturbing dreams?"

My palms grew moist. "Sometimes."

"Do you want to talk about it?"

"Is it even worth it? We've discussed this so many times." I raised my arms in frustration and let them fall in my lap with a thump.

Laura waited.

I conceded. "Okay. As you know, when I started my new job handling cold cases, I thought it would help me get over the trauma of my parents' deaths. I can't understand why the nightmares keep coming back."

"Tell me about your nightmares."

"They're vague though scary. I feel that someone who wants to hurt me is prowling nearby, but I can't see him. He's in the shadows."

"Why do you feel this person wants to hurt you?"

"I was hoping you could tell me."

"Perhaps you're still carrying guilt about your parents' deaths. You couldn't have saved them, Amber. You were a child."

"I realize that."

Laura removed her eyeglasses and placed them on her desk. "From our discussions, it's apparent that you take your work to heart. It might be affecting you more than you think."

"I agree that some of the evidence I review is horrible and violent. But I won't quit my job, if that's what you're getting at."

She joined her slender fingers. "Amber, I'd never advise you to do that. You've already told me how important your contribution is to solving cold cases and how much your superior appreciates your input."

"That's true." I didn't want to dwell on my problem any longer, so I changed the discussion to another topic. "In fact, I'm working on another case that might have a fairy-tale connection. That's partly why I came to see you today."

Interest lit up her eyes. "Go on."

I recapped the main points of Marie Troy's case, including the fact that the girl's body hadn't been found. "It might be a coincidence, but Marie was last seen wearing a red-hooded sweatshirt. It's what we call a hoodie today. 'Little Red Riding Hood' comes to mind. Could there be a fairy-tale significance in this case, like in a previous case we discussed?"

Laura leaned forward. "To begin with, the color. To the child abductor, red can represent budding sexuality and the transition from childhood to adulthood."

"But she was only eight years old."

"Precisely. She hadn't made the transition. It's one of the reasons her abductor was attracted to her."

"What? I don't get it."

She leaned forward. "You mentioned that Marie was wearing something like a hoodie the day she went missing. Correct?"

"Yes. Her mother said rain was in the forecast, so Marie covered her head with the hood before she left the house. Why?"

"Let me elaborate." Laura rested against her high-backed chair. "A woman's hair is often one of her best features. A grown woman uses it to attract suitors. If the hood covers the hair of a young girl, it conveys a message that she is not available. It signals her innocence to the abductor, who is only interested in very young girls because of their purity anyway."

I had more questions. "What would the abductor do with the red hoodie afterward? Would he get rid of it?"

"If his aim was to refine the image he wanted of his victim as untouched innocence, he would discard it. On the other hand, it's a personal choice. Another predator might prefer to keep the item as a souvenir."

A lump formed in my throat. It was possible that Ryan and I had another fairy-tale abductor on our hands. I wasn't imagining it after all.

My curiosity grew. "There's another similarity to the fairy tale in this case. On her way to school that morning, Marie visited her sick grandmother to bring her a jar of soup. We suspect she disappeared shortly afterward."

Laura aligned two pens next to the notebook on her desk. "Unlike certain versions of the story where the wolf eats the grandmother, Marie wasn't merely a victim here. She was an opportunity that the predator grabbed, perhaps by chance, to lure the little girl into his trap."

"It was daylight. I would assume someone would have heard Marie scream. Right?"

"We all know that the story of 'Little Red Riding Hood' is about a predator who pretends to be someone he is not and a young girl who is too trusting. The wolf represents the predator or the stalker. In simpler terms, stranger danger. To answer your question, one probability is that Marie, like the young girl in the fairy tale, got distracted by someone or something. Consequently, she succumbed to the abductor's invitation to stray off her usual path to school."

Anger ripped through me. I grasped the armrests of my chair. "I get that Marie was young, but it's frustrating that she was so naïve."

"Perhaps not naïve," Laura said softly. "The motto of this fairy tale is basically not to trust strangers, but children decades ago weren't warned about the sheep in wolf's clothing to the extent that children are today. It's possible that Marie's abductor didn't appear evil to her. In all likelihood, she knew this person."

"I've seen versions of 'Little Red Riding Hood' where the young girl escapes from the wolf, or a woodcutter kills the wolf."

"There was a reason for those changes," she said. "Contemporary versions of many fairy tales have been modified to end with more favorable outcomes so as not to scare children."

I had to know more. "What about a young offender? Can someone have the mindset of a child abductor in their teenage years?"

"Yes, it does happen," Laura said. "Perhaps the perpetrator was a victim of violence or exposed to violence in their youth. Statistics show that abusive incidents occur at home after school hours. Their mindset might have progressed to action during teenage years, for example, grabbing peers in a sexual way at school. Testing the waters, so to speak."

"In a previous case we discussed, you mentioned how an adult abductor might link fairy tales to his crimes. Can this apply to a much younger abductor too?"

"Yes. A ruined childhood could lead an abductor to prove that life is no fairy tale by going after children based on his interpretations of fairy tales. Like his older counterpart, the younger perpetrator abducts children to save them from a corrupt world."

Laura had once explained the perpetrator's twisted understanding of the motive behind this type of abduction. "Because he believes that only *he* can promise them a happily-ever-after ending," I said.

"Exactly."

"You once told me how pedophiles can pretend to be a nice guy, like your helpful neighbor or friendly salesclerk. It's how they fool their victims."

Laura raised a forefinger in the air. "One important fact to remember is that they normally don't change their personalities to suit the crime. Small things, like habits, usually give them away. Another point of interest is that a pedophile doesn't always act on sexual urges, whereas a child molester does."

I weighed her words. "If Marie was molested on another occasion before she was abducted, I would think she'd tell her mother about it."

"Not necessarily, especially if the molester was a family member or someone her mother knew and trusted. However, if a molester's need to kill his victim isn't satisfied immediately, the result is a state of anxiety or tension. He needs to be in control. His goal is to kill his victim as quickly as possible with no buildup to it, which would make him a murderer."

Since my time was limited, I moved on to another aspect of the case. "We're considering three persons of interest who are older men. One of them is very ill and offered a vague confession to having committed a crime, but the police have no evidence to back up his statement."

Laura steepled her fingers. "A word of caution: Don't rely solely on an old man's confession. Confusion often sets in with old age."

"Unfortunately, the pressure is on to solve Marie's case. We're at a standstill with it." I hesitated, knowing what her reaction would be to my next move. "I'd like to reach out to my old archenemy for insights."

"Vicky Johnson's abductor?" She did a double take. "Are you serious?"

"Yes."

"Amber, you know too well how abductors use manipulative methods to control and subjugate others. It's all about feeling in power and controlling. I advise caution."

"I promise I'll be careful. What I need is his expertise."

"If I understand correctly," Laura said, "you need to rely on him to help solve your case."

"If you put it that way, yes," I said.

Her brows knitted with apprehension. "You understand that this interaction has the potential to reduce your self-esteem. He can use what you say or do against you."

"How? He can't hurt me from jail."

She extended her hands in an earnest plea. "Amber, please understand that it's a psychological game for a manipulator like him. As a narcissist and psychopath, he feels no empathy but pretends he cares. He'll try to form a bond of trust with you to maintain the connection and feed his interest. He'll use mental tricks, lies, and degrading techniques to get something from you in return for favors. Above all, do not agree with him on any subject."

"I appreciate your concern, but you don't have to worry. I feel as if I know him already."

My argument didn't deter Laura from reinforcing her point. "He can manipulate you another way by not answering direct questions and changing the topic." She gave me a measured look. "I can't warn you enough. Manipulators are professional liars. In giving you false hope, it gives them a false sense of power. If you do contact him, use your rational mind, not emotions, when conversing with him."

I was adamant. "I can handle it. My psychic impressions can help me see through his shifty ways." In truth, I'll be clutching my amethyst crystal to help calm me during what I imagine will be an unnerving interaction with a serial killer.

Laura glanced at her watch. It was a sign my session was almost over.

I remembered how she was writing a thesis about the interpretation of fairy tales in today's society. She'd confided in me to guard her secret until it was published. I took the last moments of my visit to ask her about it.

"Slow progress, but it's getting there. Thanks for asking." She rose from her chair.

I stood up and grabbed my handbag. "Thanks for the advice, Laura."

"Come visit me again soon."

"I'll try." I hugged her and left.

The skies began to clear on my drive to the station. As I reviewed my discussion with Laura, I gained clarity into the big picture regarding Marie's disappearance.

Like the wolf, the abductor had refrained from kidnapping Marie until he was sure his plan would succeed. He was aware of her daily routine and how she was protected by her mother, grandmother, and friend who walked to school with her. He had to gain her trust somehow. And he did.

Now I had to gain LT's trust.

Asking for help from a man who had tried to kidnap me when I was five years old and who had succeeded in abducting and killing other little girls ran against my deepest principles. And yet, with limited resources to draw from, he could be my only chance to get into the mindset of a potential suspect in Marie Troy's case. Was I up for it?

More importantly, would Ryan approve of my bold plan?

16

———

Ryan's face flushed with anger as he stood staring at me from behind his desk. "Absolutely not!"

So much for my suggestion to interview a jailed perpetrator in person. I should have known better than to approach Ryan with a controversial topic first thing Monday morning.

I pursued it anyway. "I have to get into LT's head. It's possible that another abductor operates exactly like him."

"The answer is still no."

"Why not?"

"It's too dangerous."

Although Ryan's troubled expression indicated genuine fear for my safety, I pushed forward. "It's the only way to get information from him, and you know it."

"Maybe, but I don't have to agree with your plan. And that's final."

Standing at his desk, Matt had remained quiet until now. "Ryan, I hate to break up the party, but we have to go."

As Ryan slipped into his jacket, he said to me, "We're going out to interview potential witnesses in Louise's case. Be back soon."

~

After Matt had received permission from Louise Lavoie's sister, Nadia had prepared a page for Louise on the police website, complete with a description of the missing girl and age-progression sketches. She launched it at noon today as scheduled. It took less than an hour before she forwarded an incoming call on the Info-Crime line to me.

"I'm calling about Louise Lavoie, the little girl you're looking for," a gruff male voice said. "I saw the report about her on the police website."

My pulse picked up speed. "Do you have information about her?"

"Yes. I used to live on the same street as her. She walked in her sleep."

My pulse raced. We hadn't posted anything on the website about Louise's sleepwalking problem. "How do you know this?"

"It wasn't a bloody secret," he snapped. "Everyone on the street knew about it. Anyway, I'm a friend of the family. Her parents spoke to me about Louise's condition. Neighbors would knock at their door to warn them if they'd seen the girl on the street in the middle of the night. People began calling her the Sleeping Beauty. They didn't want to touch the girl in case they'd scare her. Her father or mother would usually get her back home and put her to bed."

Matt had mentioned how another witness had referred to the same fairy tale. I scribbled a note to ask Laura about it. "And what's the purpose of your call to the Info-Crime line?"

He let out an impatient huff. "Seeing as this case hasn't been solved, I have information that might be useful."

"Go on."

"My dog barked late one night and woke me up. I heard noise in the alley, like a vehicle had hit something. Anyway, I looked out the back window into the alley. I saw the driver get out and put something in my garbage can, then he drove away. I couldn't tell you the make of the vehicle, but I'm sure it was a gold or beige car."

The first new tip about a car! "How is this information connected to Louise Lavoie's case?" I asked.

He huffed again. "Maybe it is and maybe it isn't, but I thought I'd call anyway. You see, it happened the same night she went missing."

"Did you mention it to the Lavoie family?"

"No. Like I said, I didn't make the connection."

Something sounded off. Was the caller an armchair detective inventing clues to enrich his storytelling? I tested his sleuthing skills. "Did you look in the garbage can the next morning?"

"No," he said. "I forgot about it. While I was at work, the garbage truck went by and collected the trash."

I needed to find out more about the caller. "Why have you come forward now?"

"I'm an old man." He cleared his throat. "I've read articles about so many people going missing over the years. Police tell the public that, if you witnessed something, no matter how unimportant you think it is, it might be helpful in solving a crime. I finally got up the guts to call."

I picked up the sincerity in his voice. "Do you have any idea what might have happened to Louise?"

"She was abducted. What else could it be? Someone with an evil mind was waiting, watching for the right opportunity..." His voice trailed off. "Unfortunately, I'm afraid this story will have a sad ending."

I thanked him and logged the information, then sent a text message to Ryan and Matt.

~

Ryan hurried into the office an hour later, with Matt on his heels. Both men looked as if they were about to burst with news.

"We got your message," Ryan said. "I think we both got lucky and dug up a common piece of evidence in Louise Lavoie's case. Another witness reported seeing a light-colored car that night."

Excitement tingled in my veins. "You think it belonged to her abductor?"

"If so, it could mean a break in the case." Matt opened Louise's file on his desk. "Ryan will tell you more."

Ryan tapped his cell. "The first witness report was from an elderly woman who wasn't home the day Matt canvassed the street. She'd lived in the same area as the Lavoie family for decades. It was after midnight when she saw a girl in a white nightgown walking along the sidewalk. A beige sedan was slowly trailing her."

His revelation was mind-boggling. "You're not serious!" I said.

Ryan nodded. "Very serious. The car stopped, and a man got out. He led the girl into the car. The witness assumed it was the girl's father since there was no struggle and she went willingly. The car sped off at that point. It was dark, so the woman couldn't give us the make of the car or description of the driver."

"The second witness we interviewed had a similar story," Matt said. "Somehow I skipped interviewing him the first time around." His forehead furrowed.

I needed to connect the pieces. "Matt, was there a report from investigators about a light-colored car back then?"

Matt flipped through the pages in Louise's file. "I saw nothing about that in any of the reports. What about the witness statements in Marie's file?"

"There's no mention of a car in her file either," I replied. "Gaston drove a pickup. Eddie pushed a cart."

"What about Allen Troy?" Ryan asked me.

"There's no mention of a vehicle for him either," I said.

"Bernadette Troy or her son Tim might know what kind of vehicle Allen drove back then," Ryan said to me. "See if you can reach them."

Matt grunted. "I'm dumbfounded at how often that little girl sleepwalked down a flight of stairs in the dark of night without breaking her neck. And then she gets kidnapped. This case is so wild." He sighed. "I'll go update Louise's info on the board." Folder in hand, he ambled over to the crazy wall.

I opened Marie's file and found Tim's phone number on the slip of paper that Mrs. Troy had given us. My efforts to contact him failed, so I left a message on his voicemail.

My next call was to the retirement home. But when I asked to speak with Bernadette Troy, the front desk said she was unavailable.

"Ryan, I can't reach Bernadette or Tim," I said. "I left a message."

"Okay." Ryan rounded the corner of his desk and came up to me. He leaned in and whispered, "About what I said the other day... Don't worry, I won't share your recorded insights with Matt." To Matt who was standing by the crazy wall, he called out, "Matt, are you done?"

"I just finished," Matt said, putting down the marker. "Why?"

Ryan waved him over. "Let's compare the details of our two cases. Our brainstorming should produce new insights."

Insights. I smiled inwardly at his choice of words.

Although we were already familiar with the basic information in both case files, I suspected that Ryan agreed to go through the process to make Matt feel as if he were part of the team. What we were missing was evidence that could lead us to the perpetrator. It was a huge gap in our investigation, one that only a miracle could achieve.

17

Nadia informed Ryan the next morning that a visitor was waiting to meet with him in the conference room. It was Tim Corbin.

"Amber, come sit in on the meeting," Ryan said, rising from his chair.

I caught the quizzical look Matt gave me as I joined Ryan. I sensed he wanted to be included in the meeting, but there was no way Ryan was going to do that. Ryan and I were still the primary investigators in the Marie Troy case. Besides, Matt had already understood that we'd share any new details with him afterward.

Tim stood up as we entered the conference room. His eyes were red and puffy. "I have bad news. I went to visit my father at the hospital yesterday. I was too late." He swallowed hard. "They told me he passed away minutes before I got there."

A lump formed in my throat. Losing a parent was a difficult experience, no matter what their age. Ryan and I extended our sympathies to him.

"That's not the only reason I came here." Tim unfolded a rectangular slip of paper and handed it to Ryan. "It's a receipt from a diner where my father had stopped on the drive from Toronto to Montreal in 1968."

Ryan scanned it. "Where did you get this?"

"I found it in a shoebox where I stored mementos I'd kept since I was a kid. I swiped it from my father when he came to visit us one day. It was after my mother had kicked him out. I was four years old and loved hunting for treasures. The pockets of my father's suits were the perfect places to find them."

Ryan stared at the handwritten receipt. "It's dated the day Marie went missing, but there's no name on the receipt."

"I'm telling you it's my father's. Now you can stop pointing the finger at him. I demand that his name be cleared in connection with Marie's disappearance. That's all I have to say." He made a move to leave.

Ryan wasn't ready to clear Allen of all suspicions. "Wait, Tim. I have one last question for you. Do you remember the make of the car your father drove in 1968?"

"It was a 1966 Ford sedan. A light color, like beige or gold. He sold it after he remarried. Why do you want to know?"

Ryan shrugged. "No particular reason."

"That's all?"

"Yes." He thanked Tim for coming and escorted him out.

Moments later, Ryan pulled up a chair and joined me at my desk. He looked around. "Where's Matt?"

"I don't know," I said.

"We'll update him later. If this receipt is legit, it takes Allen off the hook for Marie's death. On the other hand, the beige car throws him onto the suspect list for Louise's."

"And you're only basing your suspicion on a beige sedan? How popular was that color in the 1960s?"

Well..." Ryan shifted in his chair. "It was very popular. There were lots of beige or gold cars on the road. What matters is that it fits in with a witness statement regarding Louise's abduction. We need to keep in mind that Allen did live in the same vicinity and, according to his ex-wife, had a questionable fondness for young girls."

I wasn't convinced. "The color of the car is too convenient an excuse to suspect him."

"Maybe, but it's a lead. Here's Allen's receipt." He handed it to me.

I studied it. "It appears to be authentic."

"Yes, it does. Then again, Allen could have obtained it from a coworker as a favor to support his alibi. Or he could have asked someone to draw up a fake receipt. It's next to impossible to verify its authenticity."

I held the receipt. An impression of a much younger Allen Corbin eating at a diner swept through my mind. "It's authentic," I whispered, then described what I saw.

Ryan squinted. "How do you do that?"

"What?"

"Sense people and places from a lousy receipt."

Nadia was gawking in our direction. Had she overheard our discussion?

I kept my voice low. "It comes through as an impression in my mind. You know that. You've already accepted what I do."

He looked away. "I suppose I have."

I let it go. Something was nagging at him, but I hadn't a clue what it was. And I certainly didn't want to make a scene with Nadia watching us.

Ryan stood up. "For the record, we can't discount Allen as a suspect yet. Period."

I watched in stunned amazement as he guided his chair back to his desk without another word. His inexplicable moodiness was one thing, but if our theories conflicted, how would we ever solve this case?

18

The subsequent hours brought renewed hope to our investigation into the disappearance of Marie Troy after the police issued a press release. The broadcast included a video reenactment of the young girl's alleged abduction in 1968. I crossed my fingers that callers with solid leads would contact us through the Info-Crime line.

Nadia and I were on the first shift. She assessed incoming calls for validity and forwarded the credible ones to me. Aside from several inquisitive callers, we received no leads. Experience taught me to be patient, that it would take more time for word to spread about the video and reawaken someone's memory, or urge someone with a guilty conscience to confess. It had happened before.

Minutes before noon, Nadia plopped a large box wrapped in brown paper on my desk. "This was addressed to you personally." She pointed to my name on the box. "It passed the security check, so it's safe to open." She hurried off.

"Thanks," I said to her back.

Ryan approached my desk. "Is that from a secret admirer?" He smiled.

Relieved to see that his attitude had improved, I replied, "Let's see." I examined the box. "That's odd. There's no return address."

He dug out a pair of vinyl gloves from his jacket. "Let's open it up."

His stash of gloves must be endless, I mused. I grabbed a pair of gloves from a box on my desk and put them on, then gently unwrapped the brown paper.

I couldn't believe it. Inside was a red hoodie! A crest with the name *BeeBee Girls Athletic Club* decorated the front of it. "What on earth... Could this be what I think it is?"

Lines stretched across Ryan's forehead. "It's either legit evidence or a rotten trick."

"There are dark spots on this sleeve." I pointed to them. "Blood?"

"Maybe. The hoodie might be contaminated by whoever handled it too. We'll send it to the lab ASAP. They might be able to get a DNA match."

As I lifted the hoodie out of the box, a note landed on my desk. I picked it up and read it out loud. It read: *Sorry I kept this for so long. I hope you find Marie's killer. Eddie D.*

"Eddie Doyle?" Ryan said, looking as stunned as I felt. "I guess he visited the police website like I suggested."

"If you're right, it means he actually cares about our progress in the case." I examined the hoodie for other marks.

"Or he's scared that we're getting close to discovering his secret."

"His secret? Are you saying—" My throat began to close. I gasped for air. I was suffocating!

Marie's face flashed before me, then spots clouded my vision. I dropped the hoodie on my desk.

"Amber!" Ryan caught me before I fell off my chair. "Breathe deeply. Breathe."

I blacked out.

No sight. No sound. My body drifted in darkness.

I slowly grew aware of muffled voices around me. Heavy footsteps from the direction of the lieutenant's office vibrated beneath me. I opened my eyes. I was on the floor! Three faces stared down at me. They belonged to Ryan, Nadia, and the lieutenant.

How embarrassing!

I jolted up. "Oh no! How long was I out?"

"A few seconds," Ryan said, taking hold of my arm.

"Easy does it now." The lieutenant took hold of my other arm as I rose on wobbly legs. He guided me to my chair, and I sat down. "You feeling better?"

"Yes, much better. Thank you."

Nadia gawked at me. "That was really bizarre, Amber. What the hell happened?" Fear spiked in her typically emotionless eyes.

I hesitated, searching for an excuse. "Um... I shouldn't have skipped breakfast this morning."

She didn't buy it. "I'm not sure about that, Amber. I mean, one second, you were holding the red hoodie and the next, you—"

"Amber needs to eat," Ryan said, cutting in. "I'll go get something for her."

"See to it, Sergeant," the lieutenant said. "I'm off to a meeting. You know how to reach me." He gave me a wary glance before he briskly walked away.

Uh-oh. I got the feeling that I was in trouble, that the lieutenant would use my physical reactions to the evidence as a reason to let me go.

But right now, I had more immediate problems.

Nadia remained glued to the spot. Judging from the way she was observing me, I hadn't satisfied her curiosity so far.

"Here, Nadia." Ryan handed her an evidence bag containing the red hoodie, the note, and the box it had arrived in. "Send this to the lab with a request for DNA analysis ASAP." As she walked away, he whispered to me, "I'll be back soon. We'll talk about this later. Try to relax, okay?"

After everyone had left to tend to their tasks, I opened Marie Troy's file. There was no time to relax. I had too many unanswered questions.

To begin with, if the red hoodie belonged to Marie Troy, how did Eddie get ahold of it?

Was he her abductor? Had he hidden the hoodie on purpose all these years to cover up his crime?

As for the note, it wasn't an actual declaration of guilt. Or was it?

If I wanted to give Eddie the benefit of the doubt, I could argue that he found the hoodie on his collection route in an alley decades ago. If so, had he conveniently forgotten to tell the police about this valuable clue, or was he simply ignorant about its connection to Marie Troy's abduction until now?

I recalled how I reacted when I'd held the hoodie. The perception that someone was strangling me was so intense that I'd blacked out. Had Marie's abductor choked her to death?

I was reviewing Eddie's recent witness statement when Ryan rushed in holding two paper bags. "Hamburger and fries from the deli across the street. Let's go eat in the conference room. It's more private there."

"Good idea." I took Marie's folder and followed him. Matt was out in the field working on leads, so he wouldn't interrupt us. Nadia was busy on the phone. Corey was minutes into his shift and scanning computer files. The lieutenant's office was empty.

Ryan closed the door to the conference room, then set his lunch down on the table. As he sat down next to me, he said, "Okay. We're alone. Tell me what happened before you blacked out."

"I couldn't catch my breath," I said. "I kept visualizing Marie."

"Strangulation. It's probably the way she died." He pulled out his phone. "I'm going to call Eddie. He needs to come down to the station for a little chat." When Eddie didn't answer, he said, "I'll try the orchard."

While he made the call, I opened my take-out bag. The delicious aroma of fries made my mouth water.

"What do you mean, you don't know where he is?" Ryan waved a hand in the air. "Yes, it's urgent. Okay. Thanks." He ended the call, then said to me, "Eddie's not at the orchard. I'll arrange to send a patrol car to his home. He'd better not be playing us."

My stomach did flip-flops at Ryan's suggestion that Eddie might not have been truthful with us. All of a sudden, my appetite vanished.

After Ryan spoke with the dispatcher and requested that a cruiser visit Eddie's home, he placed his phone on the table. "Why do I get the feeling he skipped town?"

"Why would you say that? He could be out shopping or meeting with friends."

"Or not." He took a fry from his take-out bag and chewed it.

"If Eddie did run away, I'll tell you why. He sent us a valuable piece of evidence, and what are we doing? We're hunting him down as if he were a criminal. You can be sure Eddie knew the police would suspect him after he sent us the hoodie. After all, he handled it. His DNA must be all over it."

Ryan tightened his lips. "I don't see it that way. Eddie's note could have come from a place of attrition. He's sorry for what he did and he's confessing."

"You warned me not to jump to conclusions," I said.

"It's hard not to jump to conclusions under the circumstances. The red hoodie and the fact we can't reach him indicate guilt to me." He bit into his hamburger.

His harsh analysis reminded me of Laura's theory that manipulators use mental tricks to deceive people into thinking they care. Was that what Eddie had in mind when he sent me the red hoodie? Did he expect me to believe he cared, and consequently, that he was innocent?

I had to find middle ground. "I understand that Eddie's absence and the hoodie can cast doubt about his innocence. But we don't even have a sample of his DNA on file. How can we prove he's guilty of anything?"

"We can't give him a clean slate at this point. We need to find him."

His tenacity went beyond his usual analytical views. I softly asked, "What's the matter, Ryan? You've been acting out of sorts lately."

A line formed between his brows. "I'm sorry, Amber. I tried not to let my personal problems interfere with this case, but my mom's not doing too well. The doctor said her condition was deteriorating... He spoke about a change in medication..."

His fear was palpable and sent shivers through me. I visualized his mother, her sweet smile, and her gentle manner. "I'd like to go visit your mother with you the next time. Okay?"

His eyes sparkled. "Thanks. She'd like that."

We ate without discussing his mother again. Neither of us wanted to dwell on more unpredictability in our lives.

As we were finishing our meals, a call came in through the dispatcher. A police officer reported that no one had answered the door at Eddie's residence.

Determined to play it safe, Ryan took the next step and requested that a media relations officer issue an alert for immediate release. Investigators were asking for the public's help in locating Edward Doyle who was now considered a person of interest in Marie Troy's abduction case.

Like Ryan and me, Matt worked at his desk in the afternoon, hoping that the Info-Crime line would generate helpful calls from the public. Maybe it was wishful thinking, but I was counting on Eddie, or someone connected to him, to catch the media release about him as a person of interest. Since Eddie had already taken the first step and sent us Marie's hoodie, he might be willing to talk to us again.

Our cell phones pinged simultaneously.

Ryan accessed the message and read it out loud. "The Quebec Provincial Police issued an Amber Alert. Emma Lee, a seven-year-old student at Blessed Mary Elementary School, has been reported missing." He looked at me. "Isn't that the school where your friend Nicole teaches?"

"Yes!" My senses were heightened as I retrieved the message from the QPP on my phone. I peered at the photo of a petite, dark-haired girl with a shy smile, and read on. "This girl didn't disappear from school. She was reported missing during a field trip to Eddie's Orchard." I was horrified. "Oh no! Children in Nicole's class and other classes visited that orchard today."

Matt let out a low whistle. "Don't tell me we've got a live one going around kidnapping kids from apple orchards now."

Lieutenant Payton's face was flushed as he rushed out of his office toward us. "Sergeant Baxter, the Amber Alert we just received... Isn't Eddie's Orchard connected to the case you're investigating?"

"Yes, sir," Ryan said. "Eddie Doyle is the owner. We're unable to reach him. That's why we asked media relations to issue a public alert."

"In spite of the fact that this matter falls under the jurisdiction of the QPP, and they issued the Amber Alert, it's clear that we have a stake in this search." The lieutenant's white brows gathered in a frown. "The other units are stretched thin already. Take Amber and Sergeant Gallo with you. Drive out to the orchard and find out what happened to the little girl before this becomes another cold case. A warrant will be issued by the time you get there. I'll advise the QPP that you'll be meeting up with them."

An uneasy feeling crawled over me. No child leaves a group of friends unless enticed by curiosity. Or a stranger.

What if Ryan were right? What if Eddie wasn't as innocent as I believed him to be?

One thing was clear: The recent disappearance of another child had made the situation so much worse for Eddie.

19

———

Heavy rain had filled the potholes along the back roads leading to Eddie's Orchard, making it difficult to steer the car to avoid them. Ryan swore under his breath every time he hit one, while in the back seat, Matt snickered. Had the purpose of our trip not been so crucial, I might have found their reactions amusing. That another young child, namely Emma Lee, had gone missing dampened my penchant for humor.

Soon the orchard came into view. As the lieutenant had promised, our phones pinged with confirmation of the search warrant moments before we arrived.

Ryan skidded to a muddy stop in front of the century-old farmhouse that doubled as the main building at the orchard. He cut the engine and focused on the sprawling property. "From rags to riches, as they say."

According to Corey's research data, the property boasted an agricultural spread of fifty acres, part of which was used for apple growing. Eddie shipped his apples to food retailers who stacked them in their produce aisles and produced pies and other desserts for resale. Business was good, as they say.

To the right of the main building was what appeared to be a storage area for farm equipment and tools. To the left, demolition equipment was in the process of removing a wall to provide for an extension of the premises as Eddie had told us. Six pickup trucks filled with tools and other apparatus were parked nearby. Torg Construction decals adorned the trucks, a sign of the company's continued foothold in the industry.

Relieved that I'd worn a raincoat and rain boots today, I exited the car and surveyed the drenched orchard. The scent of wet earth filled the air. As far as I could see, no one was in the orchard. Under more pleasant circumstances, my mouth would have watered at the notion of biting into a freshly picked apple. But not today. My thoughts swung to macabre theories instead, for example, wouldn't this orchard be the perfect place to bury a body?

Ryan stood on the muddied path leading to the main building, his loafers soaking up the light rain as he scanned the premises. I didn't have to ask him what he was thinking. If Emma Lee had been kidnapped, the rain would have wiped away tire tracks and other evidence by now.

Ryan gestured toward a QPP cruiser parked in front of the main building. "Let's go talk to the officer inside."

After Ryan introduced our group, a QPP officer briefed us. Slim and measuring at least six foot four, the officer said, "As you know, we issued an Amber Alert regarding Emma Lee to other local police forces. The initial hours are crucial to finding the little girl, so we're organizing a search team immediately. If she was lured away, she might still be in the area. We'll do everything we can to find her."

"We can assist you with that." Ryan mentioned he had a search warrant for the premises.

"We'll accept all the help we can get. In the meantime, we've organized a canine unit to cover the expansive grounds. She might have wandered into the forest bordering the orchard."

When Ryan mentioned our specific interest in owner Eddie

Doyle, the officer said they inquired about Eddie at the front desk and were told he wasn't on the premises. Their chat ended when the officer had to answer a call on his radio.

"I'll be around if you need to talk to me," he told Ryan before he walked away to respond to the call in private.

Ryan approached the front desk. He identified himself to the clerk and asked to see the manager.

A short stout man wearing a checkered shirt with rolled-up sleeves appeared from a side door moments later. His name tag read *Jed, Manager*. Ryan introduced us, then asked about Eddie.

"A QPP officer questioned me about him too," Jed said. "A couple of my employees saw Eddie drive away about an hour ago."

"Was he alone?'

"I don't know."

Ryan pulled out his phone and showed Jed the search warrant. "We'd like to take a look around."

"Of course."

"Did you or your staff search the premises for Emma Lee?"

"Yes, as soon as one of the teachers sounded the alarm. It was raining pretty hard out there, but my staff checked the orchard and every inch of this place. They couldn't find the kid." His forehead puckered. "I've been with the company for twenty years. Nothing like this has every happened before. We're extremely disturbed by it."

"Where are the teachers and students now?"

"In the meeting room," Jed said. "We gave them food and drink. I can take you there."

"One more thing," Ryan said. "We'd like to interview your employees and the workers from Torg afterward. Can you spread the word and make sure no one leaves here before we speak with them?"

"Of course." Jed led us through another door and down a short corridor.

Even before we got to the meeting room, the sound of children's excited voices reached us. They were fused with bouts of crying and adult voices trying to calm the youngsters.

We entered the room to find dozens of children and several teachers. Most of the children were sitting on the floor. A long table was topped with bottles of apple juice and bowls of apples, a gratuity from the orchard.

My perceptions detected a mix of emotions, and successive waves of sadness, fear, and anger rolled over me. I slipped a hand into my pocket to clutch the amethyst.

Jed raised his voice. "Can I have your attention, please?" When the noise subsided, he introduced Ryan and stated the purpose of our visit. "They'll be speaking with each teacher soon."

Nicole spotted me and made a beeline in my direction, tears streaming down her cheeks. "Oh, Amber! You have to find Emma Lee. That little girl was one of mine." Her voice trembled. "She's such a tiny child."

"It's okay, Nicole. We're here to help find her." As I put my hands on her shoulders, her distress tore through me. I quickly put space between us and slid a hand in my pocket to grasp the amethyst cluster again. I wished I didn't have to rely on it so often, but right now, the surge of emotions in the room was too much to bear.

Ryan intervened. "Nicole, let's sit down, and you can tell us exactly what happened." Over his shoulder, he said to Matt, "Start by interviewing the other teachers. I'll join you soon."

Jed collected extra chairs for us from a stockroom, and we sat with Nicole. A nod from Ryan was my cue to question her. It signaled that he believed she'd feel more at ease responding to my questions.

"Nicole," I began, "tell me when you first noticed Emma Lee was missing."

She wiped the tears from her cheeks. "We were walking through the orchard. An employee here was telling the children how the apples grow and how they get from the orchard to the store and then to the table. It started to rain really hard, so we gathered the children and took them into the main building."

"Did you check to see if all the children were present?"

"Yes, we did a head count. Twice. One of the children was missing. We did a cross-check with their names to be extra sure." A fresh wave of tears threatened to spill from her eyes. "It was Emma Lee."

"And you told the manager here about it? Jed?"

"Right away," Nicole said. "He sent his employees to look for her. They couldn't find her. We contacted the school admin and they called you. I mean, the police." She stole a glimpse at Ryan. "They also called Emma Lee's parents. They're on their way here."

Ryan glanced around. "How many teachers are in your group, Nicole?"

"Four, including me."

"I'll be right back." He excused himself and went to speak with Matt.

Nicole leaned in and whispered, "I'm so scared, Amber. If something bad happened to Emma, I could lose my job. Even go to jail." She bit her lip.

I tried to console her. "Don't blame yourself. Children wander off all the time. She can't be too far. How are the others doing?"

"Most of the children are upset because the rain spoiled their day. I had to calm down the ones who are friends with Emma. They know she's missing, and they're sad and scared. As for the other teachers..." She sniffed. "What can I say? Like me, they're in shock."

It explained the mixed emotions I sensed. Even now, a concoction of feelings kept flooding through me, and I fought to remain objective.

"Oh...I almost forgot." Nicole retrieved a child's baseball cap from the pocket of her jacket. "I found this. It belongs to Emma.

It must have got caught on a branch when she walked off." She handed it to me.

I hesitated. What if I held the baseball cap and had a horrible insight into what happened to Emma? What if I passed out again?

I took a chance. From my handbag, I pulled out a pair of vinyl gloves and an evidence bag. As I placed Emma's cap inside the bag, I caught an image of a two-story house and a little girl next to it. Nothing alarming. I exhaled with relief. Most of all, I felt that Emma was safe.

I reassured Nicole. "Don't worry. We'll find Emma."

She stared at me. "How can you be so sure? What if someone kidnapped her? I'd feel guilty the rest of my life."

I understood her remorse and placed a hand on her arm. "You shouldn't be alone tonight. Why don't you come over to my place later?"

"Are you sure? I don't want to intrude if—"

"I'm sure."

"Thanks, Amber. I need a shoulder to cry on." She noticed Ryan and Matt heading toward us. "I should be supervising the children. I'll see you tonight." She managed a brief smile before walking away.

Ryan reached my side. "We interviewed the other teachers. They didn't have much to say."

"They're in shock and feeling pretty guilty about losing a kid," Matt said. "I can't blame them."

Ryan eyed the evidence bag I was holding. "What's that?"

I handed it to him. "Emma Lee's baseball cap. Nicole found it in the orchard." I couldn't offer more details in front of Matt without revealing what I'd perceived from it.

"I'll run this over to the QPP officer," Ryan said. "I'll be right back." He hurried out.

"This is wild," Matt said to me. "I've never taken part in a cold case investigation linked to an active search for another missing kid. How do you do it, Amber?"

"Do what?"

"Deal with your feelings." He edged closer. "You do have feelings, don't you?"

I laughed off his comment. "Oh, Matt, everyone has feelings."

He didn't accept my excuse. "What I mean is, I know how sensitive you are and how emotional you get when you handle case evidence."

How did he know that?

I was relieved that he wasn't coming on to me again, yet his disclosure stunned me. I regained my composure. "I get emotional because the victims are young children. I have a soft spot for them."

Matt crossed his arms. "You don't fool me one bit, Amber."

"What are you talking about?"

"Something weird is going on with you, and I intend to—" His stopped talking when he noticed Ryan approaching us.

20

———————

Matt's suspicions about me had been cut short for now. That he'd discovered I experienced intense physical reactions to case evidence perplexed and bothered me. I was positive he hadn't witnessed any of those incidents. I was equally certain that Ryan or the lieutenant hadn't shared my secret with him. It was easy to deduct that either Nadia or Corey had briefed him.

Ryan came up to us and said, "Okay, we're done here."

"What's next?" I asked him.

His attention slid to Jed, who was standing nearby and making himself available for anything the visitors might require. "Let's go speak with Jed. We need to interview the employees and staff next. Someone must have seen something." He walked off.

Matt put a hand on my shoulder and whispered in my ear, "Our discussion isn't over, Amber."

"It is for now," I said and followed Ryan.

After Jed arranged for the interviews, Matt spoke individually with half of the orchard staff and contract workers. I accompanied Ryan while he interviewed the rest. The process went faster than we'd anticipated because the result was the same: No one had seen Emma Lee or anyone suspicious around the premises.

I hadn't captured any negative perceptions from the people we interviewed. It meant that none of them had a hand in Emma Lee's disappearance. Even so, the urgency to find the little girl overshadowed everything else.

The next phase in our plan was a visit to the storage area. Ryan asked Jed for access to it.

"Well..." Jed hesitated. "My staff already covered that area. You're wasting your time, I tell you. The QPP is about to arrive at any moment and do it all over again."

It sounded as if he were hiding something. What could be so secretive about farm equipment and tools?

"Since the missing child lives in *our* jurisdiction and we have a search warrant," Ryan pointed out, "it's necessary that we investigate every inch of this place to get an insight into what might have happened."

To be realistic, I suspected Ryan wanted *me* to get an insight into it.

Jed's cheeks grew red. "I apologize. I didn't mean to block your investigation. I thought I'd save you some time. Come this way." He led us through the office and out a door into the storage area.

I held back a gasp. The area was the size of half a hockey rink! To my amazement, there were few tools or farm equipment stored here. Instead, vintage lamps, toys, books, electronics, old furniture, blankets, and clothing stacked several feet high occupied most of the space.

Eddie was a hoarder!

A rack of old model airplanes on the left enticed Matt, and he wandered in that direction. Jed moved between stacks of items, checking for signs of Emma. He called out her name a few times. No answer.

I whispered to Ryan, "I wonder if Eddie stored everything here that he collected over the decades."

"Could be, and that's not counting the stuff in his home," he whispered back. "By the way, Emma's baseball cap... What did you sense back there?"

"I feel that Emma is safe. I perceived a two-story house."

"Do you think you can find her?"

"No, Ryan. It doesn't work like that."

He accepted my reply with a nod, then called out to Jed, "Is there access to this area from outside?"

Jed turned and headed back to us. He motioned to our right. "There's a door leading outside, but no one uses it. In fact, this section is off-limits to everyone except staff."

"I'd like to check it out," Ryan said.

Jed opened his mouth to say something but abruptly stopped. "It's over this way." He moved to the right, sidestepping piles of Eddie's accumulated items and calling out Emma's name a couple more times.

I followed Jed's example and called out to Emma. If she was scared for whatever reason and hiding in here, a woman's voice might persuade her to come forward. Despite our efforts, there was no sign of Emma.

Ryan and I followed Jed past a heaping jungle of old records, short bookshelves, and plastic bins. I marveled at the number of porcelain dolls, vintage figurines, toy trains, board games, and deflated footballs Eddie had collected.

We stopped at a massive door marked Exit.

"As you can see," Jed said, "this metal door is kind of hard for a child to open, from the inside or outside." He pushed it open. It slowly slammed back shut.

"It was unlocked," Ryan said. "Is it usually unlocked?"

Jed stared at the door as if he expected an answer from it. He turned to Ryan. "No. One of my staff must have left it unlocked after they checked the area."

I didn't get a sense he was lying. He was merely trying to cover up for someone else's negligence.

When Matt joined us, Ryan suggested we split up to continue our search. We explored the perimeter and narrow man-made paths that separated mounds of items, calling out Emma's name at intervals. To no avail.

I was disappointed. I'd expected that Emma would be found in a safe place. What could be safer than a huge space filled with children's toys, blankets, and games?

"We'd like to take a look at today's security camera system video," Ryan said to Jed.

"Whatever you want." Jed led us back into the office.

The security camera video was limited in scope. It didn't cover the new construction site or distant parts of the orchard. Trucks were seen coming and going, including two workers in a pickup truck who had finished their shift half an hour before we arrived.

"Who are those guys?" Matt pointed to the screen. "And how can I reach them?"

Jed gave him the workers' contact details. With this part of our investigation over, we thanked Jed and left the office.

At the front desk, the QPP officer was speaking with a young couple whose heightened anxiety on their faces was impossible to miss. They had to be Emma Lee's parents. Under normal conditions, I would have wanted to run in the opposite direction to avoid absorbing their angst. But I was prepared this time. Knowing that Emma would be found safe, I could detach myself from their fears.

When the QPP officer waved us over, Ryan decided that three more of us joining the conversation would overwhelm the parents, so he went solo. Introductions and a brief discussion followed. As Emma's parents listened to what Ryan was saying, their expressions brightened somewhat. I would have loved to listen in on the conversation, but Matt and I were standing too far to hear a word.

As we buckled up on the trip back to Montreal, Matt said from the back seat, "I guess this means we're back to square one. No leads until I speak to those two contractors who left early."

"It's worth following up," Ryan said, his tone light.

Although we hadn't found Emma, I sensed satisfaction emanating from Ryan. "You seem happy about something," I said to him.

He smiled. "I am. I gave the parents hope."

"What did you tell them?"

"I promised them that the police won't stop searching until they find their daughter."

Coming from someone who relied primarily on hard facts, it was a bold statement to make. But more than that, it indicated that Ryan trusted my insights.

21

———

Quebec police teams and dogs from the canine unit conducted their search of Eddie's Orchard into the early evening. While Matt left to interview the two contract workers after our visit, Ryan and I remained at the station and stayed by the phones. We were eager to get news from the QPP about Emma Lee. Any news.

Even though it was presumptuous on our part, Ryan and I were also counting on the public for a tip on Eddie Doyle's whereabouts through the Info-Crime line. We needed answers about the red hoodie he'd sent us and an explanation for his vanishing act at the orchard at about the same time Emma Lee had disappeared.

I gazed out the tall windows. The clouds had blown away, and stars sparkled in the night sky. I wanted to interpret it as an optimistic outcome for the little girl.

At the other end of the floor, Lieutenant Payton had also extended his stay, though his concerns fluctuated to the opposite end of the spectrum. He based his presence on the possibility that Emma's disappearance might develop undesirable consequences, especially if Eddie was involved. He wanted to stick around in case he'd have to answer to the higher-ups.

Ryan peeked at me from behind his computer screen. "Guess what, Amber? I googled the street address for Emma Lee's parents. They live in a bungalow. You said you saw a two-story house."

"It doesn't mean Emma lived in a two-story house. You can't decode my perceptions in a factual sense. They can be symbolic of something else."

"Like what?"

"It could mean she's in a safe place."

"Eddie lives in a two-story house, by the way."

"Pure coincidence," I countered. "Besides, the police confirmed he wasn't home. Again." Ryan had sent another cruiser there an hour ago, but without sufficient grounds for a search warrant, it had been a useless exercise.

Ryan persisted. "I think Eddie is guilty or he wouldn't have run away. The guy is an expert at hiding stuff. And himself."

"About Eddie... We have no proof that he ran away or that he's involved in Emma Lee's disappearance. Our investigation is incomplete."

"You know what? You're sounding more logical as the days go by."

I caught the humor in his voice. "You mean, more like you? Is that a compliment?"

"If you want." He laughed. "Seriously, forensics might find out more about Emma's baseball cap after they check it for DNA."

"You mean, after they compare it to *Eddie's* DNA on the red hoodie, don't you?"

"It is what it is."

Ryan's certainty about Eddie's guilt caused a ripple of doubt in me. Was I wrong to believe that the orchard owner wasn't involved in Marie Troy's abduction? And now, Emma Lee's disappearance?

No, don't do this, a small voice inside me said. *Trust your instincts.*

Matt hustled into the station, out of breath. "What a hell of a time I had tracking those two construction guys down."

Ryan asked him, "Got anything?"

Matt unbuttoned his jacket and plopped himself in his chair. "I thought the guys had driven straight home after their shift was over. I was wrong. I parked and waited an hour until they returned. Anyway, they share an apartment in one of the shabbiest quarters. And I'm being polite." His nose wrinkled. "All to say, they claim they saw nothing suspicious at the apple orchard."

Ryan sat upright. "Wait a minute. Back up. Did you enter their apartment?"

"Yes. I chatted with them, poked around. The little girl wasn't there, if that's what you're getting at."

"It doesn't mean they're not involved in her disappearance. Did you dig up their work history? Criminal records?"

"Not yet."

"I suggest you do that."

Steps thudded toward us. The lines deepening across Lieutenant Payton's forehead meant he had bad news. "The QPP search team completed their search of the grounds at Eddie's Orchard. There's no trace of Emma Lee so far. They're about to rake through loads of the owner's collectible items in the storage area." To Ryan, he said, "Sergeant, you told me your team and the staff at the orchard had searched that section. Correct?"

"Yes, sir," Ryan said.

The lieutenant took a moment to draw a conclusion. "The situation presents as a possible abduction so far."

For the second time this evening, someone had caused me to doubt myself. Was I mistaken about Emma? Would she not be found safe?

"Sergeant, have all available resources remain on standby twenty-four seven." The lieutenant thumped back to his office.

Ryan turned to me and quietly said, "Go home, Amber. Matt and I will stay here to respond to any calls on the Info-Crime line. The dispatcher will take over afterward."

I didn't argue. Drained of energy and needing to recoup emotionally, I was more than happy to leave.

~

With everything that had happened today, I'd almost forgotten about my invitation to Nicole. She knocked at my door minutes after I arrived home.

"I couldn't come here empty-handed." Her eyes were blood-shot from recent crying, yet she smiled and held out a container of chocolate ice cream.

She followed me into the kitchen where I filled our bowls with the creamy dessert. As we settled on the cushy sofa in the living room, I promised myself I'd try to remain objective so as not to absorb her emotions and throw myself into a frenzy.

I swallowed a scoop of ice cream. "Mmm...delicious. Thanks for bringing this over, Nicole."

"You're welcome." She set her bowl aside and went straight to the subject that had tormented her since this afternoon. As I anticipated, she poured out her feelings. "With each hour that goes by, I worry more and more about Emma Lee. Then I worry about losing my job. And worse. Going to jail."

My empathy for her was the catalyst that mirrored her feelings inside me. I tried not to let her grief affect me, but it was futile. I held my spoon with one hand and casually slipped the other hand in my pocket, wrapping it around the amethyst. "I'm so sorry, Nicole. But you have to trust that the police will find her."

She blinked, releasing a silent stream of tears. "If only the school would have canceled the trip, none of this would have happened."

"Why would they have canceled the trip?"

"We were short one teacher who had called in sick. The school refused to cancel the trip because they had booked the visit to the orchard months ahead and paid for it."

"If there weren't enough people supervising the children, then it wasn't your fault. Stop blaming yourself."

Nicole wasn't convinced. "We had to make sure the children didn't wander off. I can't remember if Emma was close by or with her friends a little farther away. I didn't see her wander off alone, though. Something must have distracted me." She sniffed, then wiped away her tears.

I was curious. "What distracted you?"

"That's the problem, Amber. I don't know. Maybe it was the sudden downpour of rain. I remember how we had a hard time gathering the children." A fresh wave of tears threatened to spill over.

"Kids are often distracted. And you weren't the only teacher there."

"But Emma was in *my* group," Nicole said, reinforcing the fact. "I failed to keep her safe." She reached into her handbag and pulled out a folded piece of paper. "This week, I gave the class an assignment. They had to draw an apple orchard." She unfolded the paper and handed it to me. "Emma drew this."

Green trees with heart-shaped red apples filled the page. At the top were the words, "to my *bestest* teacher." As I held it, I got an impression of a child walking with a tall man, hand in hand. The man seemed oddly familiar. *The QPP officer?* My pulse quickened as I tried to gather more details from the insight. I couldn't.

Nicole pulled out a tissue and dabbed at her eyes. "How can I live with myself if something bad happened to that child?"

Her anguish cut through me. I wished I could tell her about what I'd perceived and relieve her agony. It wasn't that I didn't trust her. She knew a lot about my private life. But if I restricted the number of people who were aware of my psychic gift, the safer I would feel. And the safer they would be too. All I could do was trust that Emma would soon resurface, and our lives would go back to normal.

My phone rang. I bounded off the sofa to grab it from the coffee table.

Happiness rang through Ryan's voice. "They found Emma."

Relief flowed through me. I repeated the news to Nicole, who burst into tears. Joyful ones this time.

"Where did they find her?" I asked him.

"In the storage area at Eddie's Orchard."

A memory resurfaced. "Remember when Jed showed us how the exit door in that area closed slowly? Emma could have entered the building after someone else had opened the door. They might not have seen her slip inside."

"My thoughts exactly," Ryan said. "Anyway, she fell asleep in the midst of gigantic stuffed animals. She was easy to miss since she's so small. According to her parents, Emma is a deep sleeper. It would explain why she didn't hear us call out. That, and the fact she was wearing headphones while listening to an old radio." He chuckled.

"Who found her?" I asked.

"The QPP officer that we met. He combed through that storage area himself."

The tall, oddly familiar man. "That's wonderful news!"

Ryan went on. "One more thing. For your ears only. Emma had fallen asleep next to a two-story dollhouse."

My heart soared with joy. "Isn't that amazing!"

He laughed. "You called it, Amber. Is Nicole there with you?"

"Yes."

"Tell her that Emma's parents are very relieved that the police found their daughter safe and sound. In fact, they won't be lodging a complaint with the school." He sighed. "I'm beat. Going home now." We said our goodbyes.

Nicole stood up and hugged me. "Thank you, Amber!" Her face beamed with delight.

"For what? I didn't do anything?"

"Yes, you did. You gave me hope that we'd find Emma." Her joy faded. "It's not over, though. Even if Emma's parents didn't lodge a complaint, the school management will decide tomorrow if I can keep my job."

"I'm positive it'll work out for the best, Nicole."

"I hope so." She grabbed her handbag. "Amber, I'm going home now. I need to sleep. I'll call you tomorrow." She hugged me again.

After I locked the door behind her, I recalled my phone conversation with Ryan. At least Emma's story had a happy ending.

But what about the other victims inside the hundreds of cold case files who were waiting for me to put their souls to rest?

Not in the least, Marie Troy and Louise Lavoie.

22

I switched gears to Marie Troy's case the next day. Her page on the police website hadn't drawn any comments from the public. I wasn't surprised. Not many people pay attention to police websites unless they're looking for specific information or are playing detective.

The highlight of the morning came when the lab delivered the DNA results for Marie's red hoodie. Ryan stood by my desk as he summarized the report and read it out loud to Matt and me. "Forensics confirmed that the blood spots belonged to Marie. The prints they lifted from the hoodie and the box it arrived in didn't match any criminal records in the database. The chemical composition of tiny fibers found inside the hoodie were assumed to be wood shavings of the sort used for bedding for small animals."

"Eddie Doyle and Gaston Belair owned dogs at the time Marie went missing," I said to Ryan.

"It's another common factor linking them to her," he said.

Matt swiveled in his chair to face us. "I hate to destroy your theory, Ryan, but lots of people own pets." He drank from his oversized coffee cup.

"As far as Marie Troy's case goes," Ryan said, "it doesn't negate the fact that Eddie Doyle had her red hoodie in his possession. He could be pretending to be a Good Samaritan by sending us the evidence."

"It doesn't mean he abducted Marie," I said. "He could have picked up the hoodie from the trash the morning she went missing."

Ryan insisted. "The only plausible suspect we have right now is Eddie Doyle. Like other perps who get caught, he could be indirectly admitting to guilt."

I crossed my arms. "Why on earth would he do that?"

"It's based on a proven theory. He wants to clean the slate in his old age."

Ryan sounded exactly like Laura. They'd probably taken the same course in psychology.

I stared at him. "Even so, we need evidence to prove Eddie is guilty, don't we?"

"Like a body," Matt said, wryly. "Let's be realistic. We've reviewed these two cases inside and out. Because of a similar MO, we suspect Marie and Louise were victims of the same abductor. I'm with Amber on this one, Ryan. Until we can prove Eddie is guilty, our perp could be any of a dozen guys on record for abductions in the same area."

I was astounded. Talk about support from an unlikely source!

Ryan raised his hands in a sign of defeat. "Fine. I'm obviously outnumbered here. I concede for now."

Matt grabbed his jacket from the back of his chair. "You two can go at it the rest of the day. I have to interview people who might turn out to be reliable witnesses in Louise's case."

Ryan gaped at him. "You've got leads in her case? You have to share this stuff with us, Matt."

Matt put on his jacket, leaving it unbuttoned to accommodate a bulging stomach. "Actually, it's more of a check-it-out thing for now. See you later." He sauntered out.

~

Nicole sent me a text message in the afternoon to say that school authorities had interviewed the teachers about the incident at the orchard. They determined that no teacher was responsible for Emma's temporary disappearance. Nicole would keep her job. She suggested we get together soon to celebrate.

Right now, a celebration was the furthest thing from my mind.

I switched my attention to the windows across the floor. The raindrops blurred my vision, reflecting the hazy information we'd gathered on the two cases we were investigating. What was I missing? To ease my doubts more than anything else, I mentally reviewed the evidence we'd gathered so far.

We had two living persons of interest in Marie Troy's case and one dead one.

While Allen Corbin was alleged to have committed an unspecified form of child abuse at a swimming pool decades ago, it hadn't been proven. Nor would we be able to clarify his statement spoken shortly before he passed away about regretting how he mistreated his children. That he drove a light-colored sedan was a notable thorn. A witness had spotted a similar car the night Louise had gone missing.

Eddie Doyle, a familiar sight in the alley behind Marie's old home at the time she vanished, was a ragman turned philanthropist with a continued passion for collecting vintage items. He'd sent us Marie's red hoodie. It was a solid piece of evidence that would label him as a Good Samaritan in my books. But if Ryan were right, Eddie was guilty of abducting Marie and merely trying to compensate for a past crime.

The witness statements we received regarding Gaston Belair, a handyman who had lived in Marie's old neighborhood, indicated that he was quiet and somewhat of a loner back then. One witness considered him a little weird. Our recent visit with

Gaston showed that he seemed to have outgrown his old habits, though. He'd become influential on the social scene by helping others to get jobs on construction projects. It was something that gave his life meaning, he'd told us.

The insights I'd perceived from the evidence on hand, although overwhelming, offered no concrete leads. Holding Marie's schoolbag, I'd perceived an unclear image of her abductor: an older, unshaven man who was still alive today. Touching her red hoodie had left me gasping for air. Was that how Marie had died?

Because of my inability to interpret my perceptions with a hundred percent accuracy, I felt as if I was failing Ryan, the lieutenant, and myself. But I was too embarrassed to admit it. A feeling of helplessness haunted me.

Why was this happening? Ryan and I had gone through the obligatory investigative steps, covered all the bases, but progress was beyond our reach. Right now, he was leaning back in his chair, gazing at the computer, twiddling a pen in his hands. If I were to guess, I'd say he was dwelling on potential repercussions should we fail to resolve current cases.

At least Lieutenant Payton had stopped hounding us. He was lapping the proverbial champagne after our efforts with the QPP at Eddie's Orchard had proved successful in finding Emma Lee. Even so, I wished we had solid facts to offer when he next asked for an update on the cold cases. Until then, I dreaded that moment.

No sooner had the thought escaped me than the lieutenant sauntered down the aisle to us. He peered at Ryan. "Anything new on those two case files your unit is investigating?"

Ryan straightened up in his chair. "Yes, sir." He briefed the lieutenant about the forensic report on Marie's red hoodie.

The lieutenant eyed me with concern. "How are you doing, Amber?"

After I'd fainted the other day, I assumed he meant my physical health. "Good, thank you."

"Where's Sergeant Gallo?" the lieutenant asked no one in particular.

"Out working on a case, sir," Ryan replied.

The lieutenant grunted. "Keep me updated." On the way back to his office, he stopped to chat with Nadia and Corey, probably to check up on their work too.

Ryan exhaled and sat back in his chair. It was a temporary relief. Based on the lack of a solid lead, we were facing a potential dead end in Marie's case and job repercussions.

It was time to discuss my proposed plan with him. Though it was a risky venture, I wanted to interview LT, one of the most notorious child abductors that Ryan and I had succeeded in putting behind bars. I'd presented my plan before, but he'd refused to even consider it.

I swallowed hard. "Ryan?"

He slid his chair over so he could see me. "Yes?"

"When I review the evidence and witness statements in Marie's case, I feel as if I'm staring into an abyss."

"No one said it was going to be easy. We can't give up."

"How can we be sure that our perpetrator is still active today?" I asked. "He's no doubt too old to abduct children."

Ryan leaned forward. "The urge could be there in his old age, but you're right that the physical ability might not."

"So where do we go from here?"

"Don't forget. We haven't cleared Eddie Doyle yet."

"What if we're wrong about Eddie?"

"Then we'll keep on investigating."

Seeing as our options were dwindling, I unveiled my idea again. "I'd like to meet with LT."

Ryan's brown eyes grew intense. "You already know the answer to that. It's no."

"Why not? He could provide more insight into the abductor's MO, like whether he continues to abduct children by hiring younger people to do his bidding. We'd be naïve to think that LT was the only abductor who built up a team to help him carry out his kidnappings."

He was unwavering. "LT is also an expert manipulator. Other felons might not be criminally intelligent, but he is. He's sly and calculating about every word he says to avoid making a mistake."

"I'm sure he'd accept my request to see him. I'll be careful in the way I ask for his help. I promise."

Ryan hesitated, seemed to be warming up to my suggestion. "He won't give you free advice. He'll want something in return. Something personal about you that he can use against you."

"I won't let him get that close," I said with resolve.

"You might not have a choice," he warned. "He'll try to get inside your head like he attempted to do before. You mustn't say anything personal about yourself to him."

"You can be sure I won't." I remembered how conniving LT was. "What can I do to protect myself?"

"Set boundaries from the start about what he can ask for and what he can't."

"Like what?"

Ryan thought about it. "Simple things are acceptable. Books, videos, cigarettes, snacks... Prisoners trade this stuff for other items."

"What if he refuses material things?" I asked.

"I doubt it. After years behind bars, these guys get greedy for outside contact. If you threaten to walk away, he'll most likely give in."

"Is that all?"

"There's one more condition." Ryan leaned forward. "I'm going with you."

"He might not open up to me if you're there."

"He might accept your request to meet with him, but I'm more experienced than you in handling these guys." He kept his eyes on me. "Are we good?"

I had no choice. "Yes."

"I'll tell the lieutenant about our plan."

"When?"

"Soon."

"How about right now?"

Ryan threw me a cautionary glance before he got up and walked over to my desk. He leaned in, pretending to view a file, and whispered, "Amber, we don't know how far-reaching LT's hold is on the outside. Guys like him don't care who gets killed and what the family implications would be. I'd never forgive myself if anything happened to you."

23

Lieutenant Payton was reluctant to grant our request to meet with LT. He eventually conceded after Ryan persuaded him that our talk with the imprisoned murderer might help us solve Marie's case.

Ryan put in a call to the Quebec jail the next morning to request a visit with LT. To our surprise, authorities approved a meeting for the afternoon. To prepare for our visit, we sat down and brainstormed questions we wanted to ask. We also chose potential items we could offer LT in exchange for information.

As we were getting ready to drive out to the penitentiary, Ryan received a call from the retirement home where his mother lived. "I'm sorry, Amber," he said, unease in his voice. "My mother is confused about her living quarters. She told the staff she wants to leave. I need to go see her right now."

"I'll go with you," I said. "We can reschedule our trip to the prison."

"No, you stick to the plan and interview LT," he said. "We don't want to risk a rebuke from him if we cancel. He might not give us another chance to speak with him."

After a brief security check by prison guards, I was led to the visiting area. I sat in one of the booths facing a glass panel that separated visitors from inmates and waited for LT to arrive.

Three seats over, a middle-aged man was conversing with a young inmate. The resemblance led me to believe they were father and son.

The door opened on the other side of the glass panel. My heart picked up speed. I slid my hand into my pocket and gripped the amethyst.

LT shuffled toward me, his large frame slightly contracted with age, and sat down. "Hello, Amber. You've grown into a fine young woman." He grinned. "How can I be of service to you?"

At the sound of his gruff voice, images of children sped through my mind like so many photos in a reel. I shivered involuntarily and clutched the amethyst cluster tighter to control the terror swelling inside me.

Without addressing him by name, I calmly said, "I need your help with a case file involving an eight-year-old girl. She was abducted in 1968."

His gaze wandered to a spot behind me. "Did you come here all by yourself to ask me that question in person? How brave of you!" He snickered, humiliating me from the start.

I ignored him. "I'm giving you a chance to redeem yourself."

"Really?" He smirked. "What's in it for me? What can you possible tell me about yourself that I don't already know."

"I might lose my job if I don't solve this case."

LT rolled his eyes. "Same old, same old. Give me something new to barter with, Amber."

"I'm serious," I said. "I might lose my job if I don't find the abductor."

"No, you won't, my little princess." His tone was sarcastic. "You know very well your uncle won't let that happen to you."

I'd almost forgotten the intimate details he'd learned about my family and me. I refused to bring my uncle into the conversation. Most of all, I hated the way he called me his "little princess." It was a deliberate reference to "Snow White," the fairy tale that had ignited his obsession with me as a child but thankfully resulted in his failed abduction.

As much as I detested the man, I didn't want to pursue the argument and lose track of my goal. "How about reading material in exchange for information?" I suggested.

A long moment of silence as LT mulled over my offer, then a sigh. "Since this is your first contact with me in my new accommodations—and I expect there will be more visits—I'll go easy on you. You can send me two of your favorite books."

His request infringed on my personal taste in reading. I agreed, knowing that I'd have to find a way around it. "Okay."

LT's sunken eyes gleamed. "Alright, let's begin. How old is your suspect?"

"He's in his seventies," I replied.

"And the body?"

"No remains have been recovered."

"His MO?"

I didn't want to disclose too much information, so I kept my reply short. "There's a possible link to a fairy tale."

A smile crept onto LT's face. "It sounds like someone I might have met. I did learn from the best, you know."

He just confirmed the existence of another fairy-tale abductor! His answer stunned and disgusted me. I took in a deep breath to settle my stomach.

When I said nothing, he went on. "Your suspect has suffered abuse as a child, either in school or at the hands of his parents."

It was nothing new. I feigned ignorance. "So?"

"He compensated for it in his later years. He created a purpose in his life, one that provided a better outcome for children than what he had experienced personally."

His idea of "a better outcome for children" had resulted in the death of his young victims. I swallowed the bile rising in my throat. "What can I do to reach him?"

More silence as LT stretched the seconds, contemplating. "Come up with a strategy that supports his abduction of the child. Something that appeals to his sense of justification."

"Justification? You mean, validate what he did?"

"In your words, yes."

"How?"

"I know you're not working this case alone," he said, belittling me once more. "Why don't you ask your partner to help you?"

I froze but recovered in the next moment. He was playing mind games, trying to make me feel incompetent by implying that someone was coaching me. I struck a confident note. "I'm asking *you*."

"Oh, come on, Amber." LT waved a chunky hand in front of his face. "I thought you were smarter than that. Surely you can dream up a plan to draw out your suspect. Admit it. Your job is at stake if you don't."

He was using and twisting what I said against me, like Ryan had predicted. I confronted him. "You said the opposite about my job moments ago."

He huffed. "You're fighting a losing battle. It's not in your best interests to ignore my advice if you want to solve the case."

He was trying to demean my efforts again.

Boosted by my silence, which he mistook for weakness in his predisposed manner, he sprinted on, peppering his words with impatience. "About what I said... If it isn't what drives your perp, it'll be what drives the next one. That's how it works. You can bet your pretty little face on it."

LT's increased pace of talking meant he was lying.

I challenged him. "The next one? What do you mean?"

He spit out the words, infuriation piercing every syllable.

"Word gets around. It doesn't matter what you do. The reality is there will always be more of them. They know you and your partner are hunting for them." He snorted. "Here's a heads-up. They intend on making your lives miserable."

I didn't have time to say another word before he awkwardly rose from his chair and hurried out.

24

Goosebumps rose along my arms after my interview with LT, though my fingers felt numb. I realized later that I'd been tightly clasping the amethyst cluster during my entire visit with him.

When I returned to the station, Ryan approached me. "How did it go?"

"Before we get into it," I said, "tell me how your mother is doing?"

"She's fine. She has these scary lapses of memory, but she'll be okay. The staff at the retirement is taking good care of her." He looked around and noticed Nadia and Corey sitting at their desks. "Let's go talk in the conference room, and you can tell me about your visit with LT."

I took Marie Troy's file from my desk and followed him. Behind closed doors, I summarized my discussion, then added, "Hearing LT's voice again brought back all those horrible memories."

"I'm sorry you had to go through this alone, but it sounds like you did great, Amber." Ryan's confidence in me was comforting.

I recalled a piece of advice that LT had shared with me. "I can't believe he actually suggested I use validation to draw in the suspect."

"He's playing you. He wants to see you fail. That's what he wants." His words weren't meant to discourage me. On the contrary, he supported me.

"Validation," I puffed. "There's no way I can approach a murderer or kidnapper and say that I support what they did. No way." I opened Marie's file and prepared to update it.

"LT's advice was interesting, especially coming from him." Sarcasm coated Ryan's voice. "As far as strategy goes, the tactic we used in the past to draw him into *our* trap is the one to beat." He gave me a thumbs-up.

"That's for sure!" I recalled my first conversation with LT after we'd tricked him into calling me on the Info-Crime line. He'd humiliated me, much like he had this time, but the outcome of the trap we'd set for him and seeing justice done had been worth it.

Ryan's tone softened. "I regret you were the bait that lured him in. You risked your life." He slid his hand under the table and briefly squeezed mine.

He was sitting so close to me that I couldn't resist. I leaned over. We were about to kiss when there was a light knock at the door.

I pulled back.

So did Ryan. "Come in." He fingered the papers in Marie's file, pretending to be busy as the door swung open.

Corey stepped inside. "Uh...sorry to interrupt, Sergeant, but I need your signature on these requisitions for supplies. It's a rush."

Ryan signed the forms. After Corey left, he turned to me with a shy smile. "We'd better get back to business."

"No kidding," I whispered, then moved on. "I was thinking about LT's advice to justify or validate a crime. It seemed ridiculous at first, but what if we used his idea in a different way?"

"Any suggestions?"

"We can flatter the suspect for his actions, instead of validating them."

Ryan's eyes flickered with interest. "You could be onto something. Narcissistic perps love to bask in the spotlight."

"We can draw public attention to their crimes through a media release," I said. "It worked before."

"We could do that but keep one thing in mind. Even if we deciphered LT's cunning ways and overcame them using a similar tactic, it doesn't mean we'll be as successful this time round with another perp."

"What if we put out a false lead to draw in the suspect?"

"Sounds good. Let's brainstorm strategies. Then we'll issue a press release." He paused. "Something else bothers me, though."

"What?"

"The danger surrounding this investigation might be worse than we think." He gave me an astute look. "If what LT said about other perps is true, your life could be in grave danger."

"What's LT going to do? Send his legions of abductors after me? They aren't exactly team players." I let out a nervous laugh.

Ryan frowned. "That's not funny."

I couldn't blame him for wanting to protect me. "You know I don't frequent strange places. And we usually go to interview witnesses together."

"I intend to keep it that way." He stood up. "Have you chosen the two books you'll send LT?"

"No."

"Don't send him anything that he can link to your personality and use against you. You know how he likes to twist things in his own sick way."

"How about a dictionary and a crossword puzzle book?"

Ryan laughed. "Perfect!"

We'd returned to our desks when Matt strutted in, coffee cup in one hand and a briefcase in the other. "Sorry I'm running late, guys. Did I miss anything?"

Ryan swung his chair around to face him. "Care to tell us what you've been up to?"

Matt placed the cup and briefcase on his desk, then plopped into his chair. "Remember those two workers from Eddie's Orchard I interviewed? Well, after I told you about my visit to their apartment, I had this gut feeling that they were hiding something. So I drove all the way back to their place yesterday. You're going to love this." He chuckled.

"What did you find out?" Ryan asked him.

"Two things. To begin with, they both had served a short jail time for petty theft."

"I thought you'd already checked if they had criminal records."

"I did." Matt reached for his cup of coffee, avoiding Ryan's stare. "Second, they got the job at Eddie's Orchard, thanks to Gaston Belair."

"Gaston did tell us he helped people get jobs in construction," I pointed out.

Ryan asked Matt, "How did those guys seem to you?"

"Like two young, fun-loving dudes looking to make extra cash. What else can I say?" Matt raised his shoulders in a shrug.

"What about their relationship with Gaston?"

"They spoke as if they were pretty chummy with him. They said they ran errands for him once in a while, like they owed him or something."

"Uh-huh."

"What?"

"Gaston told us that contractors thank him for getting them jobs by paying for his groceries." Ryan switched topics. "Anything new in the Louise Lavoie case?"

"Are you kidding?" Disbelief spread over Matt's expression.

"Give me a break. I spent the better part of the day driving out of town to speak with those two construction guys."

The friction between these two men was unmistakeable. Did Ryan expect too much from Matt? Or was he ensuring that Matt didn't slack off on solving Louise's case?

Guilt nudged at me. It was time I put pressure on myself to solve Marie's case.

25

The police spokesperson issued a statement to the media in the evening to announce that new and reliable evidence had surfaced in the 1968 kidnapping case of Marie Troy. Investigators expected to close the cold case soon.

Ryan and I anticipated that the suspect, if he were still alive, would take the bait. Or a witness from decades back might gather the courage to call the Info-Crime line. Even the faintest clue might offer a potential link to the meager evidence on hand and help us solve Marie's case. We hunched over our desks doing mundane paperwork as the clock ticked away the hours to midnight.

An unforeseen break arrived when police stopped Eddie Doyle for a driving violation late that night. After they discovered he was sought as a person of interest, they brought him to the Montreal station for questioning.

Unshaven with disheveled hair, and wearing torn jeans and a thick sweatshirt, Eddie looked as if he'd been picked up for vagrancy rather than as a person of interest. He smelled of alcohol and wobbled on his feet. Two officers escorted him to the interview room and remained on standby there.

Considering Eddie's drunken state and the unpredictable problems it might present, Ryan thought it more prudent that he conduct the session alone. I was okay with that. I could watch the process unfold on my computer through remote viewing.

Ryan sat facing Eddie across the table. He went through the preliminaries of advising Eddie that their conversation was recorded, then asked, "Have you been avoiding us, Eddie?"

Eddie raised his hands in his defense. "Hey, I took time off work. That's all. Is it illegal?"

"No. Speeding forty miles above the limit is. So is driving under the influence. But that's not why I wanted to talk to you." Ryan reached under the table for the red hoodie in an evidence bag. He held it up. "We received your delivery. Where did you get this hoodie?"

Eddie's eyes bulged. "Did you find the killer?"

"I ask the questions around here. Where did you get this hoodie?" Ryan placed it on the table.

"From a trash can."

"Where?"

"In an alley."

"Be specific," Ryan snapped. "Where and when?"

"I don't know the exact address." Eddie passed a trembling hand through his unkempt hair. "In an alley near where that girl disappeared. Marie whatever."

"Marie Troy. Eight years old."

"Yeah, that's the one."

"Why did you keep the hoodie?"

"I thought I could get a few bucks for it."

"All this time?" Ryan asked, casting doubt on him. "It's been decades since you've had it in your possession."

"I have lots of stuff from decades ago." Eddie stuck his chin out. "Valuable stuff."

"Why did you send the hoodie to us now?"

"I saw the video on TV. The girl wore a red hoodie. I remembered I had one like it. It took some time to find it."

Ryan stood up, placed his hands on the table, and leaned toward Eddie. "You sent it because you thought you could fool us, make us think that you didn't kidnap and murder Marie."

Eddie leapt from his chair. "No! That's not true!"

Ryan raised his voice. "Sit down!"

Eddie obeyed. "I swear, I didn't hurt that child. You gotta believe me." He rubbed his sweaty forehead.

Was he telling the truth? One thing was clear. He was scared.

Ryan straightened up. "We'll need a sample of your DNA."

"What?" Eddie blinked in disbelief. "Are you charging me with murder?"

"No."

"Then I don't have to give you nothin'. I know my rights."

What now? We couldn't let Eddie leave here until we'd cleared him.

Ryan was probably thinking the same thing. He changed tactic. "Eddie, did you ever own a vehicle?"

Eddie folded his arms. "I want a lawyer present before I answer any more of your questions."

The interview with Eddie had led nowhere. Despite the red hoodie in our possession, we had no solid proof that he had abducted and killed Marie Troy. Ryan detained him overnight anyway.

As we were preparing to leave the station, I said to Ryan, "Eddie might have had the means and opportunity, but we can't prove he abducted Marie. The evidence we have on him is circumstantial."

"Other serial kidnappers and killers were discovered because of one crime they committed, not *all* their crimes," he said. "Sometimes that single misdemeanor was something as simple as a cop stopping them for a broken taillight."

"So the police stopped Eddie tonight for speeding and DUI. That's quite a leap to proving he's a serial killer."

"I understand, but he's all we got so far. That's why I'm playing it safe and holding him overnight."

"It won't change anything. We can't prove Eddie abducted Marie."

Ryan held the exit door open for me. "That's to be determined. We have shelves upon shelves of child kidnapping cases to solve. Eddie could be involved in others."

His supposition didn't sit well with me. It had been a long day, and I didn't have the will or the energy to come up with a suitable reply.

Ryan's voice broke the sound of our footsteps in the near-empty parking lot. "About Eddie… Did you sense anything from him when you watched the interview?"

I opened my car door and stepped inside. "Not really. Only that he was terrified, as anyone might be when interviewed by the police. What are you going to do with him?"

"Make him sweat a little. I'll release him tomorrow. Good night." He waited until I drove away before getting in his car.

On my drive home, when I was inclined to review the events of the day, I sensed that Ryan was in a hurry to solve Marie's case. Matt had hinted as much the other day. I didn't blame Ryan. The lieutenant's pressure to increase the quota of solved cases weighed heavily on all of us.

In the end, two truths were viable in Marie's cold case. Either Eddie was telling the truth about his innocence, or he killed her and send the hoodie to the police as a smokescreen.

Which was it?

26

It was Friday the thirteenth. While this calendar date might serve as an ominous warning to some people, it started out as a regular day by my standards. That is, until the 9-1-1 dispatcher received an urgent call that morning and transferred it to Ryan.

Jed, the supervisor at Eddie's Orchard, called to report that when the crew finished the work underway and demolished the wall, they discovered human bones. The details were sparse, but Jed had already notified the QPP about it. Ryan assured him that we'd investigate the situation alongside the QPP as soon as possible.

The revelation stunned me. "A corpse!"

Ryan nodded. "It's a fluke that we have Eddie in custody, and that I haven't signed the release papers for him." He let out a sigh of relief. "The guy has a lot of explaining to do."

Doubts about Eddie flooded my mind. How could I have been so wrong about him? I'd obviously felt compassion for someone who'd managed to turn his life around. "From rags to riches," Ryan had said about him. And yet...

"Amber, I admit I might be rushing things," Ryan said, his

tone apologetic. "Although Jed told me the skeletal bones were small and looked like a child's, we won't know the identity of the victim until the forensic team steps in."

"And we don't know if Eddie was involved either," I said, upholding my initial theory.

"Right. We could have a different suspect on our hands. In any case—"

"We shouldn't jump to conclusions."

"Right again." Uncertainty about the outcome of this latest revelation cast a shadow across his face. He put on his jacket, then left to visit Eddie in the holding cell.

Will we ever solve Marie's case? With the possibility that another suspect might be involved, we'd have to switch gears and scramble to incriminate this new person all over again. It was a never-ending cycle.

Matt waltzed into the office with a coffee cup minutes later. "Anything new?"

I told him about the discovery of the corpse. "Ryan went to the holding cell to interview Eddie."

Matt's jaw slackened. "That's not possible."

"What do you mean?"

"I—" Matt's focus darted past me.

Ryan tore in as if a firestorm were on his heels. He glared at Matt. "I just found out that Eddie was released earlier. I figured it was an admin error of sorts until I reviewed the paperwork and discovered that you had authorized his release. Why, in heaven's name, did you go and release Eddie? Why didn't you confirm it with me first?"

Matt placed the coffee cup on his desk. "I came in earlier this morning. I thought I'd save you time and take care of Eddie's release."

"I'm not too busy to release my own suspects." Ryan waved his arms in frustration.

"What's the big deal? You were going to release him today anyway."

"That was before they found a body at his orchard." Ryan turned to me. "Did you tell Matt?"

"Yes," I said.

Ryan's phone pinged and he checked his messages. "Damn! I sent a cruiser to Eddie's home. He's not there." He glanced at Matt. "You'd better pray we find him. Right now, you're coming with Amber and me."

"Where?"

"Eddie's Orchard."

On our arrival at the apple orchard, we met up with a QPP officer who briefly exchanged notes with Ryan about the recent discovery of human remains. Like us, he was waiting for preliminary results from the forensic team now on-site and would arrange that they share their findings with us.

"In the meantime, let's go talk to Jed at the front desk," Ryan said to Matt and me.

"Yeah, Eddie was here earlier," Jed said in reply to Ryan's question. "He told me how he'd spent the night in a Montreal jail. He sounded off to me, sort of in a panic, so I figured I'd give you a call about what we found here."

"What about Eddie?" Ryan asked. "Where is he?"

"I don't know. He left as soon as he heard they'd dug up a pile of bones. Other workers hightailed it out of here too. I don't think they'll be back. I ordered the two workers who demolished the wall to remain on-site. I learned from experience that the police would want to talk to them." He gave Ryan their names and where they were waiting to be interviewed.

"Thanks." Ryan asked Matt to meet with the two workers while he continued to question Jed.

I was astonished to hear that Eddie had driven straight to the orchard right after Matt had released him from jail. Did he learn there was a body hidden in the wall only after he arrived here? I wanted to give him the benefit of the doubt, but running away made him look guilty. It wasn't hard to understand why he took off this time, though. He feared that the presence of skeletal remains on a property he owned might implicate him in a crime once again. And he was right.

As we stood by the demolition site, Jed motioned toward a large gap in the brick wall that had shielded human remains until now. Forensics had sectioned off the area and were performing a preliminary analysis of the evidence recovered.

Jed gestured toward the partly demolished wall. "That brick wall was first built when they expanded the warehouse years ago, so I've been told. We were planning an additional expansion, but it all went to hell this morning." He kept his focus on the wreckage site. "Unbelievable."

Ryan retrieved his phone and took notes. "When was the wall built?" he asked Jed.

Jed rubbed the stubble on his chin. "Don't quote me on this, but I believe it was built before Eddie bought the property."

"Do you know the name of the contractor?"

"I'm not a hundred percent sure, but it could be Torg Construction. They've done lots of projects like this over the last decades."

"Can you dig up that information for us?"

"I'd like to oblige, but I've got an orchard to run, and without Eddie around, I've got to do his stuff too. I don't have time to go through boxes of hard copies dating decades back and piled seven feet high." Jed raised a hand above his head.

Ryan blinked. "Decades back?"

"Most companies store records for a much shorter period," Jed said. "Eddie insisted on hanging on to all the paperwork from the day he took ownership of the orchard."

More unnecessary amassing of stuff. It made sense in Eddie's world.

Jed added, "If I'm right about Torg as the contractor, all their paper records were converted to digital files. You'll have better luck finding what you're looking for in digital format directly from Torg. Like the paper trail here, you might need a warrant. If you'll excuse me, I have to get back to my staff." He hurried toward the main building.

As the forensic team gathered their equipment and prepared to return to their lab, one of the team members approached Ryan. "Sergeant, we can't confirm the victim's gender until we run more tests in the lab. However, we can safely determine that the remains belong to a young child. The victim was wrapped in thick layers of plastic. We'll send you a detailed report as soon as we can."

A young child! This latest disclosure was like a bad movie that kept on playing. That Eddie had vanished again made him look like he had something to hide. I kept asking myself the same question: Why did he keep running away? Of course, the answer was the same, too, and so infuriating.

Matt crossed paths with the forensic team member on his way back to us. "Nothing to report out of the ordinary from the couple of workers who were on-site this morning. What did the guy from forensics say?"

Ryan relayed the news. "We need to get a search warrant for the digital records at Torg Construction. It's our best bet in tracking down the company that was hired to build that old wall."

"At least we won't have to see a justice of the peace in person to get a warrant. You got a judge you can call for a telewarrant?"

"Yes, he's on the department's contact list." Within minutes, Ryan had phoned in his request and obtained a warrant for a search of the 1968 digital records at Torg and the paper files at Eddie's Orchard. "We're good to go."

We felt confident that access to the digital information we needed would be swift. Compared with filtering through years of paperwork, digital records were clicks away. We drove to Torg, expecting that our visit would be short.

Disappointment set in when the accounting manager at

Torg told us that they only kept current records on file. "We don't maintain records going back that far," she explained.

After we returned to the car for the drive back to Montreal, Ryan called Corey. "Dig up all building permits for projects in the late 1960s that Torg or other contractors completed for the wall at Eddie's Orchard." To Matt in the back seat, he said, "This one is your baby. Your next assignment is to search through the old paperwork at the orchard. Here's where you do the real legwork."

Matt grumbled, "Why don't we wait for Corey to come up with info?"

"Here's the thing. What Corey finds might only scratch the surface. We need to find more specific information. It could be a subcontractor or an individual whose name was handwritten or typed in the body of an invoice submitted to the orchard for payment."

"That's a huge job, Ryan. Maybe Amber can give me a hand."

"Amber is working on other files." Ryan closed the discussion with a loud snap of his seat belt buckle. "We'll drive back to the station now, Matt. You can return to the orchard after lunch."

Though Matt said nothing, I sensed waves of tension emanating from him. More trouble ahead.

27

———

Nadia had handled incoming calls on the Info-Crime line while we were at Eddie's Orchard. It wasn't as if we expected an avalanche of clues from the public or anything of the sort regarding our cold cases. No, that would have been wishful thinking on anyone's part.

But Nadia's alarming call to Ryan on our drive back to the station had him speeding up our return. Judging from the anxiety in her voice, she'd received an anonymous call on the Info-Crime line that had shocked her.

As soon as we arrived at the station, Ryan and I sat down to listen to the recorded version of Nadia's conversation with the caller. That he had disguised his voice with the help of a voice-changing device was no surprise. It wasn't unusual for people to add a layer of anonymity to hide their identity when they called in.

This time, it was different.

"I know you're investigating the Marie Troy case," the metallic-sounding words rang out over the speaker.

"That's right," Nadia said.

"Stop investigating."

"What?"

"Did you know..." After a long pause, the man added, "your boss, Ryan, has a very sweet mother." Metallic chuckling.

Ryan paled.

Terror stabbed at my heart. *How does the caller know Ryan's mother?*

"Who is this?" Nadia asked.

"Put a hold on the case or you'll be sorry!"

A loud click on the line. He was gone.

"No!" Ryan said. The muscles in his neck tightened. "I'll call my mother to see if she's okay." He reached for his cell and tapped the speakerphone button.

I listened as his call bounced to the front desk at the retirement home. The attendant confirmed that Mrs. Brody wasn't available at the moment. She was with a visitor.

"Who's the visitor?" Ryan asked. "I'm her son."

There was a slight pause. "His name is Bert Noble."

"I don't know anyone named Bert Noble. My mother doesn't get visitors who haven't been cleared with me first."

"I'm sorry, sir. Security must have cleared him when he arrived."

"Thanks." Ryan ended the call. "I don't like the sound of this. I need to go see my mother in person."

"I'm coming with you." I grabbed my handbag.

With this latest threat, the mystery caller had crossed the line. It had grown beyond personal. It was ominous.

After Ryan and I signed in and showed our ID at the entrance to the retirement home, we were told Mrs. Brody was available for a visit. We hurried to her room.

My pulse quickened as we rounded the corner and reached her room. The door was ajar. I trailed behind Ryan as he rushed inside.

To my immense relief, Mrs. Brody was alone and sitting in her usual armchair. She hugged Ryan and smiled at me. "It's so nice to finally meet you, Lianne. I've heard so much about you."

"It's nice to meet you too," I said, hugging her tightly.

Ryan smiled with relief. His mother was okay. Her affection toward me also affirmed that he'd spoken with her about me, despite the name she attributed to me.

"Please, sit down." Mrs. Brody indicated the two armchairs.

Not wanting to upset his mother, Ryan gently broached the subject. "Mom, did you have any visitors today?"

She laughed lightly. "As a matter of fact, I did."

"Who?"

"A very nice man came to chat with me."

"Do you know his name?"

"No. I never saw him before."

"Can you describe him?"

"Well..." Mrs. Brody's expression went blank. "He was an older man. I don't remember much else." She smiled. "Oh...yes. He did say he was a close friend of yours. Such a nice man."

Ryan tensed up but kept his cool.

My heart pounded. I scanned the room for a gift the mystery visitor might have brought Mrs. Brody, like a box of chocolates. Anything that could trigger an impression. There was nothing more than the usual stack of books and framed photos on the coffee table.

Ryan dropped the subject of the mysterious visitor. He didn't want to scare his mother. Instead, they chatted about the weather and activities his mother had recently taken part in at the retirement home. She told us she liked to play cards with her friends and take strolls when the weather was pleasant.

When I mentioned how much I had enjoyed the books that sat on her coffee table, Mrs. Brody said, "Oh, you must come by and read them to me one day." She didn't recall that I'd read them to her during previous visits.

Although Mrs. Brody's doctor had told Ryan that her situation was worsening, I didn't see a difference from my last visit with her. I'd heard that some days were better than others for patients suffering from dementia. I imagined this was one of her better days.

An attendant's knock at the door cut short our visit. It was time for Mrs. Brody's nap.

Before we left, Ryan examined the corridor for surveillance cameras. There were none. When he asked about security measures, the attendant at the desk told him a guard at the entrance asks for ID and a signature from visitors. It wasn't much of a safeguard against intruders who could easily produce fake identification.

On our way out, Ryan flashed his badge at the security guard and asked to see today's visitor's list. The guard flipped through sheets of paper, then handed Ryan his clipboard.

A check of the signatures produced one visitor for Mrs. Brody. His name was Bert Noble.

"Can you describe this visitor?" Ryan asked the guard.

He shook his head. "I'm afraid I can't. A fundraising event here this morning brought in hundreds of people. Sorry."

This latest development had dropped us into a maze that offered no apparent exit. Who on earth was Bert Noble?

An old friend from Mrs. Brody's past that she couldn't recall?

A suspect who wanted to prove he could outsmart Ryan and gain access to Mrs. Brody as proof of his manipulative abilities?

Marie Troy's case had thrown us unpredictable curves at every turn. And it wasn't over.

28

I was convinced that Ryan and I had been drawn into a time loop. What else could explain the unpredictable events that we kept experiencing over and over?

After our visit with Ryan's mother, we were driving back to the station when Nadia contacted us with another urgent message. "A woman is waiting here to meet with police investigators regarding the Marie Troy case. The lieutenant is at a meeting at headquarters. Sergeant Gallo is searching through documents at Eddie's Orchard. Corey is out of the office. No one is available. Will you be arriving here soon?"

Nadia's tone bordered on frantic. The anonymous call to the Info-Crime line earlier had clearly thrown her usual unflappable behavior off-balance. And now, even though security had processed and cleared this new visitor, Nadia seemed afraid to be alone with her.

To make matters worse, the thunderstorm that had burst onto the city had caused traffic chaos. It increased an already congested situation as drivers attempted to access busy streets after work, bumper to bumper.

Ryan replied, "We're on our way, Nadia, give or take five minutes."

Not quite. We arrived at the station twenty minutes later to find an elderly woman sitting in the conference room, her handbag in her lap, her wet umbrella and raincoat emitting the scent of humidity. She introduced herself as Micheline Banks.

As I shook her hand, an impression of a young woman running away from a man zoomed through my mind. I managed to control my surprise and sat down across the table from her.

Ryan pulled up a chair beside me. "Micheline, we understand you wanted to speak with us about Marie Troy."

She clutched her worn leather handbag. "Yes. I saw the police reenactment video about Marie's kidnapping on the news. I felt I had something useful to share with the police who were handling the case, but I didn't want to discuss it over the phone. I wanted to speak with an investigator in person." She shivered.

"Can I get you a cup of coffee?" I asked her.

"No, thank you."

Ryan smiled, tried to put her at ease. "We're grateful that you came to see us today, Micheline. Especially in this weather."

Her clear blue eyes settled on us. "I'm seventy-three years old. It took me a while to get the courage to come here. Once my mind was made up, even the nasty weather couldn't keep me away today." Her lips quivered. "I'm sorry. I'm rather nervous. I haven't done anything like this before."

"We understand," Ryan said softly. "Can you tell us what you'd like to share with us?"

Micheline began. "I used to work for Torg Construction as a bookkeeper until my retirement ten years ago. The company was well-known all over the province. Almost everyone knew someone who worked for Torg."

Torg. Talk about a coincidence! I sensed that she had more bombshells to drop on us.

She went on. "The girls in the accounting department knew most of the workers at Torg by their employee numbers. We'd record their numbers on the invoices we sent to our clients as a quick cross-reference to the job. If one of the other girls would remark about how cute number 1631 was or how muscular number 3567 was, the rest of us understood who she was talking about. No one else did. It was an inside joke." She giggled nervously. "That's where I met Gaston Belair."

Another bombshell!

I peeked at Ryan to see his reaction.

He didn't so much as blink. Instead, he approached the subject as if the name Gaston Belair were new to him. "Micheline, does this man have any connection to Marie Troy's case?"

"Maybe." She looked down at her handbag.

Her hesitation was apparent. I was eager to hear more, but like Ryan, I waited as she gathered her thoughts.

"Gaston was a handsome young man," she said, smiling. "I dated him for a few months, off and on, like I did some of the other workers there. He didn't talk much about anything, except his work. He invited me to his home one Sunday afternoon. Several neighborhood kids were playing with his dog in the backyard. He was real friendly with them. He gave them candy, hugged and kissed them. Maybe a bit too much..." She rearranged her handbag in her lap.

Micheline was hesitant, as if she didn't know whether or not she should say more. Something was definitely up.

She continued. "I remember where Gaston used to live. It was on the same street as Marie Troy. It could have been a coincidence, him enjoying the company of kids so much, but I felt I had to mention it." Her gaze nervously darted around the room.

I asked her, "What happened to your relationship with Gaston?"

"I broke up with him," she said.

"Why?"

Micheline's shaky voice revealed fear. "I found out he was following me wherever I went. To church, shopping, lunch with a girlfriend.... Why, I don't know. It was so creepy. I couldn't wait to get away from him."

It explained my perception when we shook hands on her arrival.

Ryan stepped back into the conversation. "How did you know Gaston was following you? Was he on foot? In a vehicle?"

"He drove a pickup truck to work," Micheline said. "I hadn't noticed he was following me because he drove his father's car instead."

"Can you describe the car?"

"I don't know very much about cars. All I can tell you is that it was a light-colored sedan, like beige."

My pulse picked up speed. Ryan had said there were lots of beige or gold sedans on the road in the 1960s. What were the odds that Gaston had driven one?

Micheline went on. "I often drive by Gaston's old house where he used to live. I couldn't believe it when I saw a demolition sign on the front lawn the other day. I'm sure I won't feel as traumatized after the building is torn down."

Beside me, Ryan scribbled notes.

I asked her, "Is there anything else you'd like to tell us?"

Micheline blinked, then rose quickly and collected her things. "No. That's all."

"Thanks for coming here today," Ryan said to her. "If you think of anything else that might help us, please give us a call."

Back at our desks, I asked Ryan, "How about Gaston driving a light-colored sedan? Coincidence or what?"

"Like I said, it was a popular color in the 1960s. Tim told us his father drove a beige or gold sedan too."

"Cars aside, I sensed that Micheline was holding something back." I described what I'd perceived when I shook the woman's hand. "What I saw could have been a younger Micheline running away from Gaston. I detected fear in her to the point of panic."

"She did say he had stalked her," Ryan said. "Maybe he was the possessive type. It's not a reason to raise a red flag. He hasn't contacted her since then, right?"

His logic didn't prevent me from expanding on my theory. "What about the way Gaston was all touchy-feely with the children who played with his dog? Micheline didn't feel comfortable about it."

"According to Mrs. Troy, he allowed Marie and other kids to play with his dog. Marie's mother never complained about Gaston's behavior. On the contrary, she only had positive things to say about him."

I was adamant. "What about Sarina's witness account of Gaston? She said he was creepy too."

"I think you're making a big deal out of this for nothing, Amber."

Another perception nagged at me. "What about that flash of red and the horrible gut feeling I got when we toured Gaston's old house? Something horrible happened there, Ryan. What if Gaston was responsible for Marie's abduction? What if he buried her there?"

Ryan held up his hand. "Slow down, Amber. Now *you're* jumping to conclusions. Gaston told us he'd killed rats there. You could be picking up on that."

Rats? Maybe. Was I jumping to conclusions? Ryan just said so. If anything, I didn't want to evolve into another version of Matt, whom he considered to be too hasty in his investigations.

Ryan's attitude mellowed. "I realize we have nothing tangible to link Gaston to Marie's disappearance, but I'll keep an open mind. The same goes for Eddie, though we don't know where he is. I'll promise you one thing. When we find him, he'd better have answers to our questions."

The steps we'd taken to solve Marie's case hadn't set us on a clear path so far. The different statements from witnesses about Eddie and Gaston had further muddled our investigation. To be able to determine which one was our prime suspect required more evidence. Although I disagreed with Ryan on certain points, he was right about keeping an open mind.

Lieutenant Payton's footsteps announced his approach. "Sergeant, I understand you've been busy. Can you bring me up to speed on any developments?" He slipped a hand inside the pocket of his sport jacket.

Ryan briefed him on our interview with Micheline Banks, then said, "I thought you were at a meeting."

"It was an informal lunch with old friends." The lieutenant dismissed it with a wave. "Nadia contacted me about the Info-Crime call she received, the one that implied a threat against your mother."

"Oh, she did?"

"I knew you'd driven out to Eddie's Orchard. I didn't want to make any waves by sending a uniformed officer to the retirement home to see if your mother was all right. I cut short my lunch and went there myself."

Ryan stared at him. "*You* were the mystery visitor? Bert Noble?"

The lieutenant smiled sheepishly. "I didn't know what to expect when I arrived, so I discreetly showed my badge to the guard and wrote an alias in the visitors' book."

"Bert is short for Albert," I said. "And Noble?"

"Payton means Noble in certain countries."

"Well, that's a load off my chest." Ryan chuckled and sat back in his chair. "But it doesn't explain the anonymous call to the Info-Crime line. My gut tells me someone's been following me around and knows where my mother lives."

The lieutenant's forehead furrowed. "I understand your

concern. Best to be vigilant about your surroundings." He checked his watch. "I'll be in my office for a short while longer. Inform me of any further developments." He strode away.

I looked at Ryan. "About that anonymous caller... What if LT had one of his 'trainees' follow you, then call the Info-Crime line and threaten to hurt your mother."

He shrugged. "Anything's possible."

"What about Allen? Can we eliminate him now? Dead men don't call the Info-Crime line and threaten investigators working on Marie's case."

"Right. You made your point. However, Louise's case is another matter. Since Allen drove a beige car during the week of her disappearance, I'm keeping him on our list of possible suspects."

"What do we do next?"

"Micheline Banks mentioned a demolition sign in front of Gaston's old house. I'll call the real estate agent to ask him about it. I'll put him on speakerphone so you can listen in."

After Ryan asked him about the old house, the agent revealed that the building had already been demolished. "A crew will be cleaning up the debris soon. Sorry we couldn't work out a deal for you. As I'd mentioned, another party was seriously interested."

Ryan thanked him and ended the call.

Seeing an opportunity, I eagerly raised a suggestion. "The demolition did all the hard work for us, Ryan. It might produce clues to help our investigation. The crew should search for possible remains there."

Ryan agreed. "I'll call the demolition company. Removal of the debris can take several days. We have no choice but to wait it out. If the crew finds something questionable, they'll call me."

Though we kept running into barriers and delays, the demolition of Gaston's old house held promise. On the other hand, it would complicate our ongoing investigation if no remains were discovered there.

It meant that Eddie Doyle would linger at the top of our suspect list until he explained the discovery of skeletal remains at his orchard. But first, we needed to find him.

Would we ever connect the missing pieces?

Powerless to break the pattern, Ryan and I continued to spin around in that dreadful loop of time as unexplained findings dropped in our paths. Illusions aside, it was a promising time for the discovery of skeletal remains in unexpected places. Before the sun set, another chilling discovery would be added to our growing list.

29

The police dispatcher transferred a 9-1-1 call to our unit after skeletal remains were found in a lakeside home located in the West Island, the western part of Montreal. The constant downpour this week had flooded homes located near lakes and rivers, and sandbags had proved useless in holding back rising water levels. Damaged by the water, the walls in the basement of a decades-old home had collapsed, revealing the hiding place of a corpse.

It was almost dusk when Ryan pulled Matt off his paper search at Eddie's Orchard. The rain had trickled to a steady drizzle by the time he joined us. However remote the possibility, we speculated that the discovered remains might belong to one of our cold case victims. Grisly discoveries had their advantages in helping to solve old murders.

Police crime scene tape cordoned off the property bordering the home. On one side of the lot, forensics had set up a tent to ward off the drizzle as they inspected the remains. Matt offered to check on any progress the team had made in identifying the victim, while Ryan and I made our way to a police van to interview the occupants of the damaged home.

Mr. and Mrs. Dubois, the senior couple who owned the property, huddled under blankets provided by ambulance attendants. Police had escorted them out of their home, now considered a crime scene.

Mrs. Dubois was in shock and could barely speak. She leaned her head against her husband's shoulder, her eyes puffy from crying.

Ryan asked Mr. Dubois, "How long have you been living here?"

"Since 1967," he replied. "It was a new construction. We stayed here every summer since then. This year, it became our retirement home. We hardly had time to fully enjoy it." His eyes grew moist. Next to him, his wife dabbed at tears with a tissue as she wept silently.

Ryan went on. "Can you tell us how you found the remains?"

Mr. Dubois cleared his throat. "A few weeks ago, there was a heavy rainfall warning, so we put sandbags around the property. It happened three times over the years, but the rain was heavier and lasted longer this season. The lake overflowed and flooded our basement. We'd stored extra furniture and other belongings there. Now they're ruined." He dwelled on the thought for a moment. "The walls suffered water damage. When the water receded, I called in a repair crew to replace the wet drywall. Today one of the workers found an old metal tool box behind a wall. When we opened it up, we saw—" His wife groaned, and he put an arm around her to comfort her.

How horrifying! The anguish emanating from the couple had me clutching the amethyst in my pocket.

"Did you or anyone else touch the contents?" Ryan asked them.

"No, sir," Mr. Dubois replied. "We stepped away and contacted the police immediately."

"Do you know the name of the contractor who built your home?"

Mr. Dubois squinted. "I'm not sure. It's been so long. I think it was Torg, but I could be wrong."

When he asked his wife if she remembered, she whimpered, "No."

Matt stepped into the van. "Sergeant? Can you spare a moment?"

"Excuse us," Ryan said to the couple. He gestured that I should follow him out.

"Wait till you see what forensics found," Matt said, plodding beside us toward the tent. With every step he took in the wet grass, his sneakers made a squishing sound. If the situation had been less dismal, the noise would have been amusing.

Inside the tent, a forensic identification officer named Gregory greeted Ryan. "Sergeant, I thought you'd be interested in taking a look at this."

We approached a long table where skeletal bones were laid out in the shape of a small body.

Gregory elaborated. "A preliminary check indicates that the skeletal remains are possibly that of a child between seven and ten years old, but we need to perform lab tests to confirm our findings. The remains are somewhat preserved. They were wrapped in layers of plastic wrap, the industrial type. There was no clothing."

No clothing? The killer must have discarded the child's clothing before he encased the body in plastic wrap.

Gregory pointed toward the metal box that had held the victim's remains. "That box was located behind a wall in the home. We can assure you that the contents haven't been compromised."

While Ryan chatted with Gregory, I peered at the bones. How did these skeletal remains end up behind a basement wall? What malicious person had murdered this child? Judging from the grief I'd perceived from the Dubois couple, it certainly wasn't them.

"Cause of death?" Ryan asked Gregory.

"We'll be able to confirm that and other details after we run additional tests in the lab. We'll send you a full report."

"Thanks." Ryan handed him his business card.

I had a split second to act. My toe touched the metal box and set off a flash of red and a child's scream. I could barely contain the terror running through me. My throat tightened and I couldn't breathe. My knees buckled.

"Amber!" Ryan grabbed me, preventing my fall.

I regained my balance. "I need fresh air." I smiled apologetically at Gregory on my way out. "Sorry."

"No worries," Gregory said. "It happens all the time."

As we walked to the car, we noticed uniformed officers restraining reporters from entering the property.

"Bad news travels fast," Ryan said, sliding in behind the wheel.

"Talk about a wild discovery," Matt said as he settled in the back seat. "The owners were so freaked out."

"I don't blame them." Ryan steered the car onto the main road.

"Their story is so familiar," I said. "Eddie's Orchard made a similar discovery."

"It's too soon to get the lab results from forensics for the other set of bones," Matt said from the back seat, "but does anyone want to bet it's the same perp? Ten bucks."

I said nothing. I didn't want to gamble on such a horrible premise.

Another memory surfaced. "Remember how Eddie told us his lakeside home had flooded too?" I asked.

"Lucky he was in the construction business and able to repair his own walls," Ryan said with humor.

"Or he could have called his old friend, Gaston, to help him," I joked.

"Right." Ryan chuckled. "Like there's no love lost between those two."

Matt changed the subject. "By the way, Amber, what happened to you in the tent back there? You looked as pale as a ghost."

I froze, then said, "Oh, that. Uh...the humidity got to me."

"You don't say." Disbelief resonated in his voice. "It's weird how this stuff keeps happening to you whenever—" He stopped when Ryan's phone beeped, signaling an incoming call.

Corey's voice came over the speakerphone. "Sergeant, I have the name of the contractor at Eddie's Orchard you asked for. It's Torg Construction. The permit for the wall was issued in early 1968."

"Perfect. I have another one for you." He gave him the West Island address of the Dubois couple. "It was built in the 1960s. Torg could be the contractor."

"Do you want to hold on?"

"Yes."

Soon Corey's voice resurfaced. "City hall lists Torg as the developer for homes in that area in the 1960s. The address you gave me was one of them."

"Jackpot!" Matt said. "Way to go, Corey!"

Finally, a solid link. Excitement filled the air during the rest of the drive back as we bounced theories around.

"Torg Construction is the common denominator that can help solve our two cases," Ryan pointed out. "Gaston Belair and Eddie Doyle, our two potential suspects, worked for the company during that same period."

Matt voiced his thoughts. "There might be an employee record of them working on that wall at Eddie's Orchard."

"Then you'd better get going with that paper search!" Ryan goaded him, laughing.

"You bet." Matt snapped his fingers. "I'll be there bright and early tomorrow morning. Even if it's Saturday."

I had a broader perspective. "Ryan, I'm not rejecting your

theory, but aren't we jumping to conclusions?" I was only too happy to use his favorite phrase again.

"How?" he asked.

I explained. "First, we don't know the identity of the two sets of human remains. They might not be the victims in our two cases. Second, I doubt that Gaston or Eddie would transport a body all the way to either of those sites to get rid of it. They'd have chosen a closer or more convenient place to hide their victims."

"You're right in the practical sense," Ryan said, glancing at me. "However, desperate men will grab any opportunity to dispose of a body when it presents itself."

"Especially when it would take a bulldozer to find it," Matt said, snickering.

"A bulldozer?" I repeated. "Like the one used to demolish Gaston's old house, you mean? Wouldn't that be something."

"Third time's a charm," Matt said. "Or maybe Amber can use her magic charms to solve our cases."

I panicked. Had the staff told him about my strange experiences at work? "What do you mean?"

"Come on, Amber," Matt said. "I know how you get vibes from the evidence you—"

"That's enough," Ryan cut in. "Amber, it's okay. Tell him."

I battled between wanting to tell Matt and wanting to protect myself from what, I wasn't sure. But if I couldn't trust him, a coworker, who could I trust?

I gave him the condensed version. "I'm an empath. A psychic. I get perceptions from people, objects, and places around me. They're like bursts of images in my mind or feelings that I get."

"I knew it!" Matt said.

"Matt, you're bound to secrecy about this," Ryan said firmly. "If one word leaks out, I'll personally—"

"Don't worry." Matt's tone was serious. "I'll guard this like a secret weapon."

Revealing my gift to Matt came somewhat as a relief to me. I felt as if a heavy weight had been lifted from my shoulders. As for sharing my secret with the rest of the staff, that was a decision for another time.

As we fell silent, lost in our own musings, I mentally reviewed the evidence we had on hand for both cases. Marie Troy's red hoodie, the beige or gold car seen by a witness the night Louise Lavoie disappeared, the remains found at a lakeside home that was built by Torg Construction, Eddie and Gaston's work connection to Torg...

My thoughts backtracked to a suspect we'd almost eliminated. According to his son, Allen Corbin had driven a beige car. Although he had died, could he still be considered a feasible abductor in Louise Lavoie's case? Ryan had said so, while I'd maintained that the color of the car was a convenient excuse to keep Allen on our suspect list.

Despite suspicions about our three potential suspects, we didn't have solid evidence to incriminate any of these men. But it was early yet. The lab tests from forensics could determine their fate. As well, the demolition of Gaston's old house might yield unexpected results.

Above all, I believed in my gift. Despite the rare glitches, my perceptions had been correct in the past. I intended to go forward with the same resolve.

30

———————

I regretted having to cancel my reading visit to General Hospital and the retirement home on Saturday, but it was crunch time at the station. Even the lieutenant dropped in to get a recap of our progress. While Matt was tracking down specific documents at Eddie's Orchard, the rest of our team put in extra hours catching up on paperwork and taking incoming calls on the Info-Crime line. The media had already spread unconfirmed reports about the possible discovery of remains at the lakeside home, increasing the number of calls from cranks.

The highlight of the morning arrived with a report from forensics that identified the remains discovered at Eddie's Orchard. A DNA analysis confirmed they belonged to Marie Troy. The gold ring on a chain that Marie had worn provided solid evidence to support the conclusion. A tiny envelope containing the jewelry was included with the report.

Standing next to me, Ryan held out the envelope. "Do you want to give it a try?"

A glance at the other end of the floor confirmed that Nadia was on the phone, and Corey's attention was fixed on his monitor. "Shouldn't we use the conference room for privacy?" I whispered.

"The lieutenant is in there. His glass-paneled office won't give us privacy either."

"Okay." As soon as I took the envelope, a tightening sensation around my throat seized me. I dropped the envelope on my desk and almost passed out before I could reach the crystal in my pocket. Ryan was close enough to prevent my fall. I grabbed his arms to steady myself.

Apprehension filtered Ryan's words. "Amber! Are you okay?"

The dizziness passed. "Yes."

Nadia had hurried up to us, unnoticed till now. Her voice pierced the air. "Are you really okay, Amber? I saw what happened. What the hell is going on here?" She glared down at me.

"Nothing," I said, wishing she'd leave.

"That's the second time this weird thing has happened to you."

Actually, it had happened more often than that, but I didn't correct her.

"Nadia, let's not make a big deal out of this," Ryan said.

She put her hands on her hips. "Not a big deal? What if Amber is sick? Passing out like that isn't normal."

Why was she talking about me as if I weren't there? "It's okay, Ryan. It's time the others find out."

He threw me a cautionary look. "Are you sure?"

By now, Corey had joined us. "Find out what?"

"That I'm empathic, that I sense things and capture images from people and objects," I said. "What I perceive from crime scene evidence can be difficult to take sometimes."

Hesitation registered in Nadia's eyes. "Are you joking?"

"No, she's not," Ryan said.

Corey chimed in. "So Amber, you're not a real police consultant."

Ryan came to my defense again. "Yes, she is. Without Amber's help, this unit would be at a standstill. If fact, without her, there would be no unit today, and you guys wouldn't be working here."

"Who else knows about this?" Nadia asked.

"Aside from us, the lieutenant and Matt." Ryan wasn't finished. "Let's keep it that way. We can't afford this leaking out to other departments, least of all to the public. We need to consider Amber's safety. The last thing we want is a loser finding out and stalking her."

"Message taken, Sergeant," Corey said. "My lips are sealed." He padded back to his desk.

Nadia's lingering stance told me she wasn't totally convinced. "Even if what you do seems mindboggling to me, you should have told us. We can keep secrets, you know." She crossed her arms.

"It was a decision taken at the highest level," Ryan said. "Are we good here?"

"Yes, Sergeant." Nadia returned to her desk.

"I'm glad we straightened that out," Ryan whispered. "Let's hope they keep their end of the deal." He pulled up a chair next to mine. "Want to tell me what you experienced when you held Marie's jewelry?"

I sat down and shared what I'd seen and felt. "It was similar to what I'd perceived at the lakeside property. How is that possible? The skeletal remains there obviously belong to a different victim."

"Like we discussed before, if it's the same MO, it's probably the same perp. Statistics indicate that perps display routine in the way they dispose of their victims."

"You feel confident that we're closing in on him?"

"After your insight today, yes." Ryan's phone rang and he answered. It was Matt.

"Hey, guys!" Matt roared over the speakerphone. "Guess what? I found legal documents that show Eddie purchased the property in 1968. There's more. In the payables, Torg Construction is the company most often recorded on invoices to the orchard in 1968. Many of them have vertical numbers listed in the body of the invoice. No idea what those are."

"They could represent individuals or subcontractors who worked on a project for Torg. A code system of sorts."

"Does this mean I'm finished here?" Matt asked.

"No," Ryan said. "We need more evidence. You have to decipher those numbers. Look for a vendor list, like numbers that cross-reference to company names or individual contractors."

"I haven't found any records like that so far."

"Keep searching."

"Anything new at your end?"

Ryan briefed him on the lab report for Marie Troy, then ended the call.

"That's promising news from Matt," I said. "I wish forensics would get back to us about the identity of the remains found at the Dubois property."

"We should hear from them by Monday," Ryan said.

"What if the remains belong to Louise Lavoie?"

"That's to be determined."

"Should we consider a copycat killer?"

"Statistics say otherwise." Ryan leaned in and spoke in a quiet voice. "Amber, are you okay to make the call to Mrs. Troy about her daughter, or would you like me to do it?"

"I'll do it."

He returned to his desk, leaving me to mentally prepare myself before I called Bernadette. How does anyone tell a mother that her daughter's remains have been found and that the discovery would be broadcast on the evening news tonight for everyone to hear?

When I relayed the news to Bernadette, her reaction was calm. "Thank you for letting me know. It's what I thought had happened to Marie all these years. She can rest in peace now."

I sensed that Bernadette would finally experience that peace too.

After Matt strolled into the office an hour later, he suggested a tactic that tested Ryan's patience. I sat by, listening.

"If we put the discovery of Marie's remains on Louise's web page," Matt began, "it'll show there's a possible connection to the same killer. People might call in with clues."

"Not a great idea," Ryan said.

Matt scowled. "Well, I think it's a great idea. Doesn't my opinion count for something?"

"Here's the thing," Ryan said. "If we do that, it might compromise both investigations. By the way, we're issuing a press release tonight about the discovery of Marie's remains."

"Will you link it to Louise's case?"

"No."

Matt grunted in frustration. "Then how do you expect me to solve this case? I want to post clues on our police website to get the public involved, and you're cutting me down at every turn."

"You'll have to find another way. We don't want to scare off the perp, especially if it's the same one in both our cases."

"But—"

"What we don't want to do is publicize information that also has the potential to motivate a copycat killer. Are we clear?"

Matt nodded reluctantly. "I'll find another way."

It was after eight that evening when our team headed home. As arranged, a dispatcher from the homicide department took over the Info-Crime line and would forward any incoming calls to Ryan.

Emotionally drained from the week's events, I needed to restore my psychic energy. In essence, I needed sleep. Ryan was understanding, and I admired him for respecting my space. We agreed we'd get together tomorrow—Sunday.

On the drive home, the sensation that someone was watching me crawled over my skin. I checked the rearview mirror. A pickup truck was driving behind me, but his headlights blinded me so that I couldn't see the driver.

I accelerated. The truck accelerated.

My heart pumped faster. I needed to get out of this dilemma and not lead the driver to my doorstep.

I took a side street that I normally don't take to throw him off my trail. It worked. I sped home the rest of the way.

Relief washed over me when my house came into view. I pushed the button on my remote to open the garage door. As it slowly closed behind me, I relaxed and wiped the perspiration from my forehead.

Was this job finally getting to me?

31

———————

A loud crash jolted me awake at dawn. At first I thought an earthquake had caused a vase to topple from the dresser beside my bed.

A cool breeze flapping the curtains confirmed otherwise. Something had broken the window!

I stepped out of bed onto the hardwood floor. "Ouch!" I removed a tiny piece of glass from under my foot. I scanned the floor and noticed a rock the size of a grapefruit.

Stepping into my slippers and avoiding the debris on the floor, I cautiously pulled the curtains back to peek outside. No movement. Whoever had broken the window was long gone.

I was about to reach for the rock, then remembered to pull on a pair of vinyl gloves first. I picked up the rock. An elastic band held a note in place around it. The message read: *Stay away or die!*

As I held the rock, the shadowy figure of a young man throwing an object whizzed through my mind, then vanished. I tried to recover it, but like most of my perceptions, the glimpse was time limited.

I fumbled for my phone on the bedside table. My hands trembled as I hit Ryan's speed dial.

"Amber?" His groggy voice was music to my ears.

"Someone flung a huge rock through my bedroom window!" I blurted. "A threatening note is attached to it."

"Are you hurt?"

"No. Just scared."

"Make sure all the doors and windows are locked. I'll be right over."

I checked all the locks on both floors. Then I splashed water on my face and got dressed.

Soon Ryan rang the front doorbell. He locked the door behind him, then hugged me tightly. He put space between us and placed his hands on my shoulders. "Are you sure you're okay, Amber?"

"I'm fine. My bedroom window needs a repair job, though."

"Let me take a look."

I led the way upstairs to my bedroom. I hadn't had time to clean up the fragments of glass. "Watch where you step."

Ryan surveyed the damage. "Where's the rock and the message?"

"Over there." I pointed to my dresser where I'd placed the items inside a transparent evidence bag.

He picked up the bag to get a closer look. "Did you see who did this?"

"No." I told him about my perception. "I couldn't see the young man's face, but the message on the note can't be any clearer."

"We must be getting close to solving our cold cases," Ryan said with confidence. "And to finding the perp."

"Maybe one of our suspects hired this man."

"It's highly possible. I'll get this rock to the lab after I board up your window. I saw a piece of plywood in the basement the last time I was here. I'll get a hammer and nails and cover up the window temporarily."

After Ryan had completed the task, he stood back to survey it. "There. That should do for a while."

"Thanks. I'll call a company on Monday to replace the broken window."

He slipped his arms around me. "We can't ignore this latest threat. You understand that I have to notify Lieutenant Payton about it, right?"

"I understand, but I'm afraid of the consequences."

"What do you mean?"

I shared my fears. "What if he takes me off the case? Or worse. He lets me go."

"I doubt you'll lose your job over this," Ryan said. "We just need to protect you better."

"How?"

"You could benefit from having a personal bodyguard for a few days."

"You know the lieutenant won't approve more expenses."

"Who said anything about expenses?" He smiled.

"Oh. You mean *you*?"

"Why not? You can stay at my place, or I can move in with you here. Your choice."

I hesitated. It wasn't as if I didn't have an extra bedroom to accommodate him. Nor would he be moving in permanently with me, like other couples did when their relationship got serious. Not that our relationship had reached that stage. It was far from it. What Ryan was offering was a short-term, preventative measure to put me at ease. So why was I overanalyzing the situation?

Another obstacle surfaced in my mind. "What if Lieutenant Payton doesn't like the idea?"

Amusement edged Ryan's tone. "We don't have to tell him. No one knows about our relationship anyway."

He was right. "Okay. You can stay here."

"Thanks." He planted a quick kiss on my lips. "I'd better get going. I'll drop off the evidence bag at the lab. Then I'll grab an overnight bag from my place. See you later."

After Ryan left, Nicole called and asked if we wanted to get together today. I'd forgotten that it was my turn to have her over at my place.

"Oh, Nicole. I'm sorry, I can't. I worked yesterday, and I might have to put in more time today."

"No problem," she said. "I called you at the last minute, just in case. I understand how unpredictable your job can be. We'll plan something for next weekend."

After we said our goodbyes, I felt horrible. I hated lying to her, but how could I enjoy myself when someone had threatened my life moments ago?

The press release about the discovery of Marie Troy's remains hit TV and social media Sunday evening. The public was referred to the Montreal Police website page for more details about the alleged abduction in 1968. They were also encouraged to call the Info-Crime line with any information that might lead to the arrest of the perpetrator.

"If there's one thing that surprised me," I said to Ryan as we sat in the living room after dinner, "it was how calm Bernadette was when I called to tell her about her daughter."

"She probably cried afterward," Ryan said. "It's as if we opened an old wound again."

"She sounded grateful, though. I felt peace emanating from her when I spoke with her. I'm glad she can close the book on that part of her life now."

He put his arm around my shoulder and said softly, "Amber, if I didn't know any better, I'd say you were speaking from personal experience."

"Maybe I am." I smiled at him. "Except for the peaceful part."

He squeezed my shoulder. "I'm here now. You don't have to worry about an intruder."

I was thankful that Ryan provided me with a sense of security, but it was short-lived. He'd go back to his home in a couple of days. Nothing removed the fact that my attacker would be lurking out there, waiting to pounce on me at any moment.

And I'd be looking over my shoulder until he was caught.

32

Comforted by the fact that Ryan occupied the guest bedroom of my home Sunday night, I slept soundly till the next morning. His promise to watch over me the next few days put my mind at ease too.

Ryan's suggestion to stay over hadn't been such a bad idea after all. As we'd agreed, we didn't mention our temporary living arrangements to anyone, not even to family or close friends. Our jobs would be at risk if word ever reached the lieutenant. Most of all, we didn't want anyone to draw incorrect conclusions about our relationship. It wasn't close to the serious level that someone might assume.

Ryan drove out to the station before I did. He had an early morning meeting with homicide detectives about cases he'd worked on before he was transferred to the cold case unit.

The timing was perfect. I'd planned on visiting Laura again and needed an excuse to leave an hour before my shift began at the station. Now I was free to go there without having to lie to Ryan. I preferred keeping Laura's existence a secret. She was my backup source of information, a reliable specialist who helped me link child abduction cases to fairy tales.

At eight o'clock, Laura welcomed me in. "You're looking rested, Amber. I assume life is treating you well?" She sat in the high-backed chair at her desk.

"In general, yes." I took a seat across from her.

"I can only chat with you a short while today," she said. "I have a staff meeting soon."

"I'm sorry. I should have called you."

"It's okay. If we run out of time, you can always come back. You know how much I enjoy seeing you." Her smile and mannerisms reminded me so much of my mother and the friendship they'd shared.

"I like coming here too," I said. "The last time I was here, Laura, we spoke about a case I was working on. A red hoodie was involved."

"Yes, I remember. We discussed a possible connection to the fairy tale, 'Little Red Riding Hood.'"

"That's right. Well, there's been a new development in the case. A red hoodie was delivered to the police station. Forensics confirmed it belonged to the victim, Marie Troy. We believe her abductor sent it. He's one of our suspects."

Laura positioned the pens alongside her notebook. "That's interesting."

"Even more interesting is that a note was included. The sender expressed hope that the hoodie would help the police find Marie's killer."

"Have Marie's remains been found?"

"Yes, recently. Why?"

Laura leaned forward. "As you already know, manipulators love to brag about their achievements. Use it to your benefit."

"You think he's bragging that he's the abductor by sending us the red hoodie?"

"It could be interpreted as such, but my assumption is not a verdict of guilt. You'll need to go through the usual investigative process to prove that."

Something nagged at me. "If the abductor did send us the red hoodie, why would he do it now, decades later?"

"Criminals sometimes open up a Pandora's box of secrets and reveal their crimes. They want to make a fresh start or wipe the slate clean."

Ryan had voiced the same theory. "Why would they want to reveal their crimes?" I asked.

Laura sat back. "In the case you're investigating, the abductor might be old or terminally ill. If he believes in the afterlife, acknowledging what he's done is a way of coming to terms with it. Do keep in mind, however, that perhaps he isn't quite ready to brag about it."

"Why not?"

"He could be playing a game to see if he can outsmart the police first."

I moved on to the next topic. "Another cold case we're investigating hints at a fairy tale too: 'Sleeping Beauty.'" I explained how a witness had described Louise Lavoie, the nocturnal sleepwalker, in a flowing nightgown and how the young girl seemed to glide down the street. "What can you tell me about the type of abductor who links this fairy tale to a potential victim?"

Laura grew pensive. "To begin with, statistics indicate that child abductors have low self-esteem. Accordingly, they have a difficult time with female relations. Most abductors are single men, though some are married and have even raised families. They can be distant with people and are largely perceived by others as weird. In relation to the tale of 'Sleeping Beauty,' the abductor sees the young girl as pure and innocent. He believes that she has been waiting for him to arrive and remove her from a charmed sleep."

"How?"

"'Sleeping Beauty' represents the awakening of the feminine principle, or gentle energy, that was put to sleep. The abductor imagines that he is her true love and can awaken her by his kiss. 'Love conquers all' could well be his motto. This delusion guides him to believe that he can give the young girl *a happily ever after.* And we both know where that leads."

"Yes, unfortunately."

Laura glanced at the tiny clock on her desk. It was a sign that my time was over.

I stood up. "Thanks, Laura."

She walked over to me. "It was good to see you again, Amber." She hugged me before I left.

Later that morning, word came in from the crew inspector concerning the demolition of Gaston's old house. The debris had been cleared away. Nothing suspicious had been found, which meant that Ryan and I faced another dead end.

I'd been wrong to expect that the demolition would expose the remains of a body in Gaston's former home. Despite witness statements describing Gaston as "creepy," our suspicions about him as a likely suspect in our abduction cases had now all but vanished.

Even so, I couldn't forget the flash of red I'd captured during a visit to his old home. Something violent had happened there, and it had to do with more than his claim that he'd killed rats. I was certain of it.

Ryan shared his theory with me. "It doesn't mean Gaston didn't abduct Marie or Louise or anyone else," he pointed out. "It could mean he chose another place to get rid of them."

"I noticed you didn't include Eddie or even Allen. Why not?"

"We're talking theories here. I could have named any other suspected child abductor that frequented the same geographical area." He wasn't finished. "To be clear, Eddie and Allen are still in the picture too."

I raised my hands in exasperation. "So we're back to square one with three suspects."

"So far. That's where Matt's legwork comes in. If he deciphers the numbers on the Torg invoices, we might discover who worked on building the wall at the orchard."

I remained firm. "Which eliminates Allen. He didn't work in construction."

"True, but he might have abducted Louise and hidden her body elsewhere," Ryan said.

My frustration mounted. "We're going in circles. We don't even have the results from the lab for the skeletal remains found at the lakeside home. They could belong to a victim other than Louise."

"I agree. The crazy thing is, we might even uncover the identity of a totally different killer in the process." His phone rang and he answered.

I took advantage of the break in our conversation to calm down. Our cold cases had remained unsolved for years, even decades. A few more days wouldn't make a difference. I needed to focus elsewhere.

I opened up Marie's file again. The feeling that I'd missed something had troubled me for days. My instincts were driving me to find any morsel of information that would guide me in the right direction. If we couldn't prove who killed Louise, I would at least try to eliminate Allen as a suspect.

I picked up the tattered photo that Bernadette had given us when we interviewed her. In the photo, a young woman is sitting on an unmade bed in her underwear, a dreamy look on her face as she stares at whoever is taking the photo. It was easy to assume the photographer was Allen. On the reverse was her note addressed to Allen: *Thanks for tonight, from your Toronto love, Debbie.* Beneath it was a handwritten date: *October 31, 1967.*

Halloween! It was the same day that Louise Lavoie had gone missing! Matt had even joked about it.

Looking at the picture again, I spotted a digital clock on the night table next to the bed. I hadn't paid attention to it until now. I used the magnifying glass on my desk to get a sharper view of the clock. The display read 11:30 p.m.

I rushed over to Matt's desk and opened up Louise's file. The investigator's report stated she'd gone missing between midnight and two in the morning.

My mind whirred as I did the math. Allen couldn't possibly have driven from Toronto to Montreal before Louise went missing. It was a six-hour drive, which meant he hadn't arrived in town before five in the morning.

What a relief! We could finally eliminate Allen as a suspect in Louise's disappearance.

Ryan had ended his call.

"Look at this!" I showed him what I'd discovered.

He gave me a thumbs-up. "Good job. I'll let Matt know."

I had to interrupt our discussion to take a call that Nadia transferred to my desk. It came from a maximum-security prison in the province of Quebec.

My pulse raced. I knew of only one person who was serving jail time there.

"Thank you for sending me the books." LT's hoarse voice sent shivers down my spine.

I tried to sound detached. "It was our agreement."

"Ah, yes. I'll treasure the notion that your mind works like a giant maze and is accessible to many possibilities."

Unbelievable! In his own twisted way, he tried to adapt my personality to the puzzle book and dictionary I'd sent him.

"By the way, I caught the newscast about one of your investigative cases the other day." He laughed. "Amateur hour at its finest."

I refused to ask LT to explain. It would be like asking him for a favor again. I pretended I wasn't interested in his comment and said nothing.

"Keep in touch, my princess." A click at the other end.

My blood went cold. Had I opened a door that should have remained closed forever?

33

Sitting at my desk, I briefed Ryan on my recent conversation with LT. "What did he mean by 'amateur hour'? Was he referring to our investigation?"

"Exactly. He took the opportunity to insult us, like he did in the past. You know how much he enjoys creating conflict. Let it go, Amber. We'll show him a thing or two when we nab our perps." A ping on his computer screen diverted his attention. "Forensics sent us a report."

I stood up. "What does it say?"

Ryan scanned the document, his eyes reflecting growing interest.

As I watched his reaction progress to a smile, my patience evaporated. "Come on, Ryan. Share. What does it say?"

"The remains discovered in the wall at the Dubois lakeside home belonged to Louise Lavoie."

"So it was Louise." Relief, then sadness, enveloped me. "Remember the insight I had about choking in a dark place?"

"Yes. You called it, didn't you?" Ryan gave me an appreciative look.

"We need to find Louise's killer," I said. "If we could find evidence that would point to—"

"Speaking of evidence, it's past noon. Has Matt been in touch with you lately?"

"With me? No. Why?"

"He hasn't called in and isn't answering his cell." His phone rang and he glanced at the display. "Speak of the devil. I'll put him on speakerphone."

"Sorry, guys," Matt said. "I overslept. I had a late start this morning at the orchard."

"You could have called in," Ryan said.

"I figured it would be alright, seeing as I put in extra hours on the weekend."

"We *all* put in extra hours on the weekend."

Matt huffed in annoyance. "Anyway, I found invoices that Torg billed to the orchard for the wall. I'll send you the copies. I haven't found a vendor list that cross-references the numbers on these invoices to names yet."

"It's okay. You're making progress. By the way, we have news about your case." Ryan briefed him on the lab report for Louise Lavoie.

Matt let out a low whistle. "We're finally getting somewhere. I'd better get back to work."

"Keep me posted." Ryan ended the call, then tapped buttons on his cell. "Amber, can you take a look at the invoices that Matt sent? I forwarded them to you."

"Sure." I downloaded the files.

"In the meantime, I'll go brief the lieutenant about the latest lab report." He made his way to the front office, confidence in his stride.

I examined the invoices for projects that Torg Construction had completed in 1968. As Matt had mentioned, random numbers were listed in the body of the invoices billed to Eddie's Orchard. Who did those numbers represent?

Two numbers came up often for the project on an interior

wall at the orchard. They were 2222 and 4603. A handful of other invoices indicated EZ followed by a number. Even with this new data, I needed names to go with those numbers.

Then I had a eureka moment!

When Micheline Banks had visited us at the station, she'd described the accounting aspect of her job at Torg Construction. She'd used a system that linked each employee or subcontractor on a project to an exclusive number.

Relying on Micheline's memory for answers, I phoned her. I cut through the initial chitchat and asked her about the two numbers on the invoices.

"Oh, we had so many people working for us over the years," she said, "though one of the numbers you mentioned stands out. It was 2222. I clearly remember the name that went with it because he did a lot of work for Torg." She paused. "It was Gaston Belair."

My breath caught in my throat.

"The other number belonged to Eddie Doyle," she added.

Eddie Doyle? Of course. He'd worked there long before he bought the orchard. Even better, Gaston Belair had referred him for a job at Torg in the first place. Work buddies. Interesting.

"What about these other numbers?" I ran off five other listings that began with the letters EZ.

"That was EZ Build, an internship company that worked for Torg," Micheline said. "The workers were high school students who did small repair jobs at the orchard. Nothing major."

Not important. I scratched EZ from my list and thanked Micheline for her help.

I sat quietly, grateful that the former Torg employee's memory had narrowed our list of suspects. The frequency of two familiar names popping up on the invoices was difficult to ignore. As much as I'd judged Eddie to be a decent person, my doubts about him and Gaston were now on equal footing.

Ryan returned to his desk. "Find anything?"

I couldn't hide my enthusiasm. "And how!" I shared my newfound evidence.

"Here's the thing. Micheline's memory is a helpful clue, but we need solid evidence. There's no way to confirm that information without access to the vendor files at the orchard." He rubbed his forehead. "You know, I never thought it would come down to this, but I have to say it."

His downcast demeanor worried me. Was he admitting defeat? "What?"

"Solving this case depends entirely on Matt."

"Do we really have to wait for Matt?" I asked him. "We're running out of time. We need to come up with a different plan."

Ryan's expression brightened somewhat. "We would need a foolproof strategy to lure in our suspect. We've done it before. Any ideas?"

"We can release a press report about updated findings in Marie's case."

"I'm listening."

"We can claim our suspect worked on a project for Eddie's Orchard the week she went missing."

"That approach is too direct. We'll have all sorts of crazies calling in. We need to come up with another tactic. Something less personal."

I recalled LT's advice. "If Eddie calls in, we can play a game with him like LT suggested. Make him feel as if we approve of the crime he committed."

Ryan nodded his head so-so. "It could work, but it means we're relying on Eddie to call us. He might not take the bait. What about Gaston Belair?"

"It's a different situation," I said. "We know how to reach him. We can call him."

"We need a pretext for the call."

What evidence did we have on Gaston, except for the fact that he'd worked at Eddie's Orchard? Like in Eddie's case, it was circumstantial at best. "We could question Gaston about his time working at the orchard...pretend that we need his help...ask for information."

Ryan considered it. "Interesting points. Our call might stir him into action if he thinks we're onto him. If we go with this plan, we need to use someone in the police ranks. It'll make the call to Gaston official. I know someone in homicide who fits the bill. Let's go for it." He raised a thumb as a sign of acceptance.

We presented the aspects of our plan to Lieutenant Payton and waited while he digested it. If there was ever a moment for a speedy decision, this was it.

The lieutenant agreed without wavering. "I'll arrange with homicide to supply you with the required manpower and technical support," he told Ryan. "Best you evacuate the staff and get Sergeant Gallo out of the orchard before you set your plan in motion. I can't afford to lose any member of this unit." His gaze shifted from Ryan to me. "Stay safe."

After we returned to our desks, I said to Ryan, "That went so much easier than I thought it would."

"Yeah, too easy." He tightened his lips.

"What do you mean?"

"Why do I have a feeling that Matt is going to be a problem?"

"Let's call him," I said.

After Ryan put Matt on speakerphone, he updated him about our impending sting operation. "You need to instruct Jed to make sure everyone vacates the orchard by four o'clock today. That includes you."

"But it's only three o'clock," Matt said. "I'm not done. I'm telling you, Ryan, there's no way I can get through the rest of the paperwork in an hour."

"Listen, Matt. You have to leave by four o'clock. It's a direct order from the lieutenant."

An impatient huff at the other end. "Fine."

A sinking feeling drifted over me. It wasn't a reaction to Matt's pigheadedness or his cheekiness. Those were passing irritations. It was rather a sense that the secret plan we were about to initiate held nothing but danger for us.

34

———————

At four o'clock, Matt called Ryan to confirm that everyone had left Eddie's Orchard. "All done. I'm the only one here."

Ryan gave Matt our location so he could join us there. "We'll see you soon."

We waited, but Matt didn't show up. Our efforts to contact him failed and went to his voicemail.

"Something tells me he's still at the orchard," I said.

"If you're right, I'll deal with him later," Ryan said between clenched teeth. "Right now, the teams are standing by, waiting to put our operation into action."

Timing was everything. As soon as our press release update about Marie Troy was broadcast in the early evening news, calls to the Info-Crime line started to pour in. I wasn't surprised. Based on visitor statistics that Corey had gathered, her reenactment video and her page on the police website had already attracted public interest.

What prompted an increased public response this time was that the police suggested a link between Marie's disappearance and the remains discovered at Eddie's Orchard, a familiar tourist attraction. The mention of such a connection was guaranteed to cause more than a ripple effect.

While public interest in Marie Troy's case was astounding, Corey and Nadia reported that incoming calls ranged from unusual to outright disturbing and offered nothing noteworthy so far. They would reroute any important calls to Ryan or me off-site where we set up our covert maneuver.

Since Eddie's Orchard was located in a rural area under the jurisdiction of the QPP, Ryan notified them of the operation. They offered to assist our surveillance team and we accepted. Ryan chose a single-room motel close to the orchard as a command post where technical officers connected phone apparatus to recording devices.

Sitting at a table in the motel, Officer Leo Pilon instigated phase one of our plan. He phoned Gaston Belair at his Montreal home.

Ryan and I stood by, listening, counting the rings at the other end. Although an officer had confirmed that Gaston hadn't left his home all day, our plan depended on him answering the phone.

A male voice boomed, "Hello."

Officer Pilon introduced himself. "Is this Gaston Belair?"

"Yes."

"I'm investigating a criminal case with Detective Sergeant Ryan Baxter. We understand that you once worked at Torg Construction."

"I already told the cops that I worked for Torg."

"Company documents indicate that you worked on a project at Eddie's Orchard in 1968."

Gaston grunted. "I worked on a lot of projects there. Who the hell can remember that far back?"

Irritation peppered his words. I took it as a sign that our tactic was working in our favor.

Officer Pilon went on. "Perhaps I can refresh your memory.

You worked on a project involving a wall to expand the warehouse. Do you remember that?"

Gaston hesitated. "Uh, no."

"Can you confirm what your employee number was at Torg Construction?"

"I don't remember."

"Your employee number at Torg was 2222. Is that correct?"

Gaston raised his voice. "I already told you I don't remember!"

Officer Pilon kept his voice even. "It's alright, Mr. Belair. We'll check with the accounting department at Eddie's Orchard. They must have a copy of the invoice that listed your employee name and number on it."

Silence from Gaston.

"As I mentioned earlier, I'm working with Detective Sergeant Baxter on a cold case. In connection with that file, I'm calling to notify you about a recent discovery of human skeletal remains at Eddie's Orchard. Would you know anything about—"

A loud click.

Officer Pilon looked at Ryan. "He cut the connection, Sergeant."

"That's fine, Constable." Ryan smiled at me. "Gaston took the bait."

"Do you think he'll get there before us?" I asked him.

"No. Our motel is a short drive from the orchard. All we need now to support our suspicions is the right paperwork. And Matt."

"Do we know where he is?" I asked.

Lines crossed Ryan's forehead. "I haven't heard from him, and I can't reach him. I'll try one more time." After another attempt, his call went to voicemail. He left an urgent message. "Last call, Matt. Leave now!"

I hadn't been able to shake the feeling of dread that had enveloped me earlier. "Matt could be trouble."

Ryan scowled. "He will be if he stayed at the orchard after I ordered him to leave. Our teams have already surrounded the place. Our sting operation is in the works right now."

An urgent call was transferred to us from the Info-Crime line. It was Eddie Doyle. Officer Pilon recorded the conversation.

"I know you're recordin' this conversation," Eddie said. "I saw the news about Marie Troy and how you linked her disappearance to my orchard. I'm really mad about that. The bad publicity is goin' to kill my business."

Was that all he was worried about? His business? What happened to the Good Samaritan who had sent us Marie's red hoodie?

"Come down to the station, Eddie," Ryan said. "You must be fed up, especially after so many years of not getting the proper recognition for what you've done."

Ryan stunned me. He was playing the game that LT had suggested.

Eddie chuckled. "Are you kiddin' me? You still think I did this, don't you? I didn't even own the orchard then."

"You worked on construction projects at the orchard before you purchased it."

"Maybe. I don't remember the exact dates. What difference does it make? What the hell proof do you have that I killed that kid anyway?"

Aware that it might be his last chance to lure Eddie in, Ryan said, "Your employee number is recorded on an invoice from Torg Construction to the orchard. The project you worked on was a wall during the week Marie went missing. You know all about it already, don't you? You were there when the demolition crew discovered her remains."

"I have nothin' more to say to you," Eddie retorted.

The line went dead.

35

———

In an impromptu secret operation, Montreal and QPP officers surrounded Eddie's Orchard but ensured that public access to the property remained open. The open road would persuade our suspect to drive in.

Police teams kept surveillance from behind clusters of trees and shrubs. Equipped with a two-way radio earpiece and microphone, officers surveyed the main building and the area surrounding it. Their weapons were at the ready, in case a potential intruder was armed.

Ryan had sent each officer photos of our two suspects, Eddie Doyle and Gaston Belair. Uncertain if Matt was on the premises or not, Ryan had also circulated his colleague's photo to establish his identity so they wouldn't mistake him for a suspect.

Hidden in a clearing behind a clump of trees, with huge boulders forming a protective shield behind us, Ryan and I had a clear view of the main building. But time was running out.

Ryan looked up at the sky. "It's getting dark. Soon we won't be able to see much."

All of a sudden, an explosion sounded from the main building.

"What the hell?" Ryan listened to an update through his earpiece and repeated it to me. "There's smoke at the back door of the building. An officer is moving in to check it out." He peered through the trees. "There's no visible damage to the front of the building."

I peeked out between the branches. The front door to the main building burst open. Matt rushed out!

"Hold your fire! He's one of ours!" Ryan said into his microphone.

In his hurry, Matt tripped. He got back on his feet and ran, though he was slightly off course.

"Over here!" Ryan shouted.

Matt adjusted course and clambered through the trees into the clearing where we stood.

"What the hell happened?" Ryan asked him.

Panting, Matt said, "Someone blew up the back door... I took off." He thrust a business envelope at Ryan. "It's all in there. Our suspect worked there...hid the body behind a false wall. We got him."

Ryan skimmed the contents of the envelope, then said to Matt, "You were right when you first made the connection between the abductions of Marie Troy and Louise Lavoie."

Matt smiled. "Thanks, Ryan. That means a lot to me."

Ryan handed me the envelope. "This is the only proof we have. Guard it with your life."

Another explosion rocked the ground!

We dropped to our knees. Ryan shielded me, protecting me from scattering fragments. When it stopped raining debris, we rose to our feet.

"That was damn close." Matt wiped dust particles from his shoulders. "Talk about wild!"

Ryan listened as a surveillance officer relayed a message in his earpiece. To us, he said, "Flames are soaring from the main building. Firefighters have been dispatched."

"They blew up the place," Matt said, grinning nervously, "but I got out with the evidence."

"We'll discuss that later." Through his mic, Ryan ordered police officers to approach all entrances to the main building, including the storage depot on the left and the entrance to the equipment dock on the right. "Amber, stay here." He turned to Matt. "You okay to come along?"

"You bet!" Matt followed him through the trees.

I opened the envelope and scanned the contents. It was exactly what we'd been looking for: proof that our suspect had been working for Torg at Eddie's Orchard the week Louise Lavoie disappeared. I folded the envelope and tucked it in my pocket.

I should have been surprised, but I wasn't. My insights had pointed in his direction, from his past interactions with children to his pretense in wanting to helping others less fortunate. The fact he'd casually referred to Ryan as my boss should have raised a red flag, but I'd missed it. It was a term he'd used when he'd anonymously spoken with me on the Info-Crime line.

The perceptions that I'd captured about Marie Troy and the suffering she'd endured before her death were fresh in my mind. I pictured the fragile little girl, hurt and bruised. That someone could dispose of her body in such a horrid manner made my stomach turn.

I stared through the trees, hoping to catch a glimpse of the action, but the team had vanished into clouds of black smoke and rubble. They'd no doubt entered the building by now. They might have even rounded up Marie's murderer.

A feeling of dread abruptly overcame me. I sensed a presence behind me and spun around.

Gaston Belair stood there, aiming a gun at me. Malicious vibes emanated from him.

Terrified, I froze and stared into the face of evil.

"Did you really think your cop friends could catch me?" He smirked. "I know this area like the back of my hand. It was so easy to slip by them."

I wanted to run, but my legs were glued to the spot. Even so, I was no match for a merciless killer with a gun.

"One of the cops stole a document from the orchard. Give it to me." He took a step toward me and put out his hand.

I winged it. "I don't have it."

"I was hiding behind those rocks back there." He motioned over his shoulder. "I saw and heard everything."

If Gaston was hiding nearby, someone else must have broken into the building and detonated it. It meant he had one or more helpers.

"Give me the document," he repeated.

"No!" I took a step back.

"Do it, or you won't see another day."

"Not so fast," a familiar voice shouted from the left.

Eddie Doyle!

Before Gaston could react, Eddie pounced on him. The men struggled, twisting and turning on the ground, each trying to gain control of the gun.

Their powerful emotions overwhelmed me. Waves of hate, jealousy, revenge, and greed swelled from them, invading my space. Aware that a stray bullet could hit me at any moment, I looked for an escape route.

The only way to safety was the path back to our police cruiser. But was that path any safer, what with Gaston's accomplices lurking around?

A shot rang out.

Gaston groaned and fell to his knees, the front of his shirt drenched in blood.

Eddie held the gun with both hands and maintained a shaky aim at Gaston. "You won't hurt the children anymore. Your killing days are over."

Bushes stirred beside me. "Drop your gun!" Matt commanded, his gun aimed at Eddie.

Eddie let his gun fall to the ground and held his hands up.

Two officers rushed in and handcuffed Eddie.

"No, not him!" Matt said. "Cuff the other guy." He turned to me. "You okay, Amber?"

"I will be." I exhaled, releasing the tension inside me.

Gaston Belair was sentenced to jail for the murders of Marie Troy and Louise Lavoie. When the police interrogated him, he mentioned how he'd wanted to keep the ring on a gold chain that Marie had worn as a souvenir, information that investigators had withheld all along. He changed his mind just before he hid her body in the wall structure at Eddie's Orchard late one night.

Police arrested two young men who had assisted Gaston in his plot to destroy company records at the orchard. His assistants, the ones he'd eased into jobs there, were the same men that Matt had driven out of town to interview. They eagerly tattled to the police that Gaston had paid them to blow up the orchard. In return for their confession, they received a lighter jail sentence.

Eddie Doyle was acquitted in self-defense. As for the destruction at the orchard, he claimed the property was insured, and the blast had solved his hoarding habit. He promised his staff that they would remain on payroll while the orchard would be rebuilt.

When we asked Eddie where he'd been hiding out, he admitted he was at a neighbor's farm minutes away, waiting for Gaston to strike. "That guy passed me a fast one, tryin' to blame me for his crimes," he said. "I made sure he'd never do it again."

That Matt had neglected repeated warnings to leave the building didn't escape Lieutenant Payton's attention. "Sergeant

Gallo, when a superior officer gives you an order in the future, you must comply. Be forewarned. If this happens again, I'll have to consider taking disciplinary measures."

Lieutenant Payton's reproach didn't stop him from showing how pleased he was about our unit's recent success. Aside from proudly briefing the higher-ups at headquarters, he personally showed his appreciation when he invited our team to dinner at his home one weekend.

In a reference to Gaston Belair, Matt said at one point, "To think that all it took was an employee number on a job invoice to catch him. It was one for the books." He chuckled.

"To borrow the timely advice a convict once gave us, we validated his work," Ryan joked, adding to the word game.

"I've got one," I said. "His number was up."

More relaxed than usual, Corey and Nadia joined in the banter, naming technical terms that had double meanings. The sense of camaraderie was uplifting.

I felt at ease. Everyone in the unit had accepted me, in spite of my different approach to the job. I did catch the occasional lingering stare from Nadia and Corey, though, as if I were an odd specimen of sorts. Were they wondering if I could read their minds?

Maybe one day I will.

ACKNOWLEDGMENTS

Like the first book in the Amber McNeil Mystery series, *The Red Hoodie* was inspired by a fairy tale. During my research, I came across experts who claimed that, although fairy tales often present surreal dilemmas, they help us to interpret danger and solve problems. It was with that mindset and my love of fairy tales that I launched this series.

I wish to thank the beta readers, editor, and cover designer for their valued suggestions and comments. A special thank you goes to my family and friends who continue to support my writing endeavors.

My gratitude extends to readers whose feedback lifts my spirits and motivates me to write more stories in the genres I love. I am humbled by your continued interest in my work.

ABOUT THE AUTHOR

Sandra Nikolai is the author of the Megan Scott/Michael Elliott Mystery series and the Amber McNeil Mystery series. In addition to her novels, Sandra has published a string of short crime stories, garnering awards along the way.

A graduate of McGill University in Montreal, Sandra held jobs in sales, finance, and high tech before leaving the corporate world to pursue a career in writing. She likes to think that plotting a whodunit reveals the lighter—yet more mysterious—side of her persona.

Visit www.sandranikolai.com and sign up for Sandra's quarterly newsletter to get news on book releases, exclusive offers, and other inside information. Your email address will never be shared and you can unsubscribe at any time.

You can also find Sandra on

Twitter: twitter.com/SandraNikolai

Facebook: facebook.com/SandraNikolaiAuthor

Instagram: instagram.com/sandranikolaiauthor

ALSO BY SANDRA NIKOLAI

Amber McNeil Mystery series

The Missing Slipper

Silent Night

Megan Scott/Michael Elliott Mystery series

False Impressions

Fatal Whispers

Icy Silence

Dark Deeds

Broken Trust

Cold Revenge

For more details, visit Sandra's Book page on her website at
www.sandranikolai.com